"JOSHUA!" THOR CALLED
AS HE STRUGGLED
IN SKRYMIR'S GRIP.

"Get back to Valaskjalf! Tell Odin what's happened!"

Skrymir grinned. "Why bother? I've ordered my armies to march on Asgard. He'll know soon enough."

Joshua glanced at Jarnsaxa. "Go!" she cried. "There's nothing you can do here!"

Joshua nodded and ran for the chariot with Lincoln at his side. A shadow came over him, and he knew that a giant hand was reaching for him. It clapped down over him like a cage.

VOYAGE OF THE BASSET

THOR'S HAMMER

BY WILL SHETTERLY

Random House ⌂ New York

For my fellow members of the Sacred Flying House:
Rachel Brown, Emma Bull, Alex Epstein, Kay Reindl,
Doselle Young, and Janine Ellen Young

www.randomhouse.com/kids

Library of Congress Cataloging-in-Publication Data
Shetterly, Will
Thor's hammer / by Will Shetterly.
  p. cm. — (Voyage of the Basset ; 4)
SUMMARY: In 1876 San Francisco, three boys from very different backgrounds are
rescued from drowning by a magical ship that takes them on a quest to Asgard,
home of the Norse gods.
ISBN 0-375-80274-6
[1. Magic—Fiction. 2. Adventure and adventurers—Fiction. 3. Mythology, Norse—
Fiction.] I. Title. II. Series. PZ7.S55457 Th 2000 [Fic]—dc21 00-59114

Printed in the United States of America   December 2000
10 9 8 7 6 5 4 3 2 1

Cover illustration by James C. Christensen.

CONTENTS

VOYAGE OF THE BASSET

THOR'S HAMMER

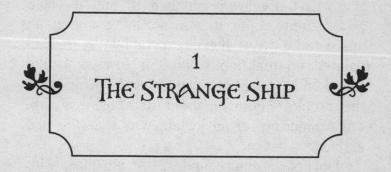

1
THE STRANGE SHIP

No one saw the ship sail into San Francisco Bay one winter day in 1876. It came during the quietest hour, when thieves and smugglers had gone to bed because dawn was close, and farmers and fisherfolk still slept because dawn had not yet come. It slipped through the thick night fog so easily that its crew must not have needed eyes to find their way. It tacked so closely into the breeze that its sails must have been filled by some force other than wind. It slid so silently beneath the prows of larger ships that you would have sworn there was something supernatural about it.

And you would have been right.

Later, as the city woke, no one along the waterfront—not seamen and dock workers in their rough clothes or visitors and passengers in their finery—wondered about the ship as it lay at the wharf. Everyone noticed it, and if you'd asked them about it, you would've gotten an answer like "Aye, there's an odd little ship all painted up that looks like Sir Francis Drake sailed on it. Has *Basset* painted on its prow." And they would've gone on about their business without wondering for an instant why the ship had arrived.

Docked among modern steamships with their great side paddles and fast clipper ships with their towering masts, the ship looked even smaller. Its high prow and high stern made it seem as if it had sailed directly from the sixteenth century into the nineteenth. Its bright colors made it look as if it belonged to a rich band of circus performers.

On its high stern, the first mate said, "Who've we come for this time?"

The captain tugged on his beard. "Can't rightly say."

"It's a secret?"

"No. I don't have a name. Only a time and a place: here, at noon."

"San Francisco's a busy place. There'll be plenty of people here at noon."

"True enough."

"So what's the passenger look like, then?"

"Good question. I wish I knew."

The first mate turned and stared at the captain. "So how'll we find the one who needs us?"

The captain smiled. "We're here. Whoever needs us will find us."

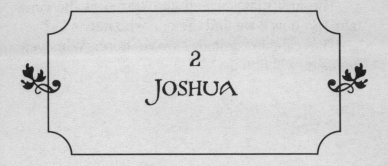

2
JOSHUA

Joshua Green woke as something warm and wet slapped back and forth across his face. He didn't need to look to know what it was. Laughing, he said, "Stop it, Lincoln!" He didn't expect that to have any effect, but it did—the gray mongrel licked his face even faster.

Joshua brought his arms up over his head and rolled across the hay pile. The old dog followed, lowering his broad head to nuzzle and lick as if he were still a puppy—a huge, shaggy puppy with very bad breath.

"All right, already!" Joshua laughed again, pushing the dog away. Light was streaming through the cracks between the boards that made the stable walls. At any instant, Old Man Carter would be coming around to see if Joshua had begun the morning's chores.

He stood and brushed hay from his clothes: jeans so thin that the wind laughed at them, and a jacket with a button for every buttonhole, but no two buttons matched. He untied the strings that served as laces in old shoes his grandmother would have called "so holey they're downright sacred." He shook hay and dust from those holey shoes, carefully rewrapped his feet in the sheets of newspaper that served as his socks, then tied his shoes back onto his feet.

Lincoln yipped at the door. It opened a moment later. Old Man Carter stepped in, squinting into the dark stable as he scratched the stubble on his cheek. "You awake, boy? Get you some chores done, and the old lady'll have biscuits and eggs waitin' on you."

"I'm up, Mr. Carter," Joshua replied. "I'll get right to it."

The old man grunted in acknowledgment and walked away. For a white man, he wasn't too bad. In the month that Joshua had lived there, Old Man Carter had never hit him. And while no one would ever mistake the food Old Lady Carter fed him for something good, it was filling, and it was the same food that the Carters ate.

The morning chores at the stable consisted of shoveling out dung from each stall, filling the water troughs for the five horses and the cow and giving them their morning hay, milking the cow, spreading grain for the chickens, and gathering the eggs. It took time, but it wasn't hard work, not like farm labor during planting season when he wrestled a plow all day, or during harvesting when he was constantly bending over to pick something, like strawberries or cotton. He supposed he should count himself lucky.

Milking was Joshua's favorite chore. The milk steamed as it squirted into the bucket, and the cow's soft teats felt warm in his cold hands. To ease his thirst, he gave himself a shot of fresh, hot milk. One swallow made him feel stronger and more awake.

He could have drunk all that the poor cow had to give, but neither the cow nor the milk were his to keep. He contented himself with the squirt for himself and one for Lincoln. The old dog was so startled when the milk hit his head that he took three steps back, sat on his rump, and whipped his head angrily from side to side to shake off whatever had hit him. Then he realized what it was as the milk dripped into his mouth, and barked for more.

When Joshua had finished all of the chores, he carried the milk and eggs to the back porch of the Carters' small whitewashed house. He called, "Mr. Carter? I'm done."

Old Lady Carter came to the door. Usually she was a hard-faced, suspicious woman, but this morning, she smiled at him. "Come on in, Joshua. I kept a plate warm for you."

"Thank you, ma'am." He turned to Lincoln. "You stay, hear?"

"I got something for that critter, too," said Old Lady Carter.

That surprised Joshua even more than her smile. The Carters did not do anything that they considered wasteful. Feeding useless strays was wasteful, they had said more than once, so food for the dog had always come from Joshua's plate, or from the occasional penny or two that he took to the butcher for fresh bones and meat scraps.

Old Lady Carter put a plate of burned corn bread down by the door. Lincoln looked suspiciously at her—he had been swatted with Old Lady Carter's broom more than once. But when she did nothing, he poked his nose into the blackened corn bread and began gulping it down.

"Thank you," Joshua said for the dog.

"I woulda just tossed it out, anyways. Wasn't paying no mind to what I was doing, and I burned the whole mess," said Old Lady Carter. "You come on in, Joshua."

Wiping the thin soles of his shoes against the boards of the porch, he wondered what her kindness meant. Sometimes he had fantasized that the Carters would take him in and give him a

room and three meals a day in exchange for helping them. The Carters were old, and their children had moved away. They needed help. Joshua
needed a place where he would be appreciated.
He told himself that he wanted too much, but his
hope grew as he followed Old Lady Carter into
the warm kitchen.

Old Man Carter sat at the table, sipping a cup
of tea. He looked up at Joshua and said, "Boy, you
been a hard worker. We noticed that."

"I can work hard," Joshua agreed. "I've had
practice."

"I'm sure you have," said Old Man Carter
with a grin.

Old Lady Carter put a plate of eggs, grits, and
corn bread on the table before him. "Careful of
that plate. It's hot from the oven."

"Yes, ma'am." Joshua stared at the food, but
he hesitated to sit. All the time he'd been there,
he'd always eaten alone, either in the stable with
the animals or in the kitchen after the Carters
had finished.

"Sit and stuff yourself," said Old Man Carter,
and Joshua could hear kindness under his gruff
tone. "Don't want it cold, do you?"

"No, sir, Mr. Carter." Joshua sat and looked at
the plate heaped with food, then at the tidy
kitchen. He could get used to this. He began to
eat. The grits were runny, the eggs were hard,

and the corn bread was dry, but they tasted delicious. He smiled at Old Lady Carter. "I appreciate this, ma'am."

"Glad to hear it," said Old Lady Carter. She
looked at Old Man Carter in a pointed way, so
Joshua looked at him, too.

The old man worked his lips, like he wasn't
sure what to say or do, then reached into his
pocket and slapped a silver dollar on the table.
"What do you think of that?"

Joshua looked at it, not knowing what to
think.

Old Man Carter laughed. "Go on, take it.
That's yours. I told you we saw you were a hard
worker."

"And we came into some good fortune," said
Old Lady Carter, "so we wanted you to share in
it."

Hope leaped high in Joshua's chest. "Thank
you." He picked up the coin. He'd had his share
of five- and ten-cent pieces, and even a few
quarter-dollars, but he couldn't remember a
dollar of his own. His entire family had worked
on people's farms for only a couple of dollars a
week. "I don't rightly know what to say."

"Your face said it all," said Old Lady Carter,
smiling.

"We sold this place," said Old Man Carter.
"Stinson from down near the wharf came by last

night, said he wanted to expand and he heard we'd been thinking of going back east. So that's what we're doing. We'll catch the train next week, but they're taking the animals today."

The words didn't make sense to Joshua. If the Carters were leaving, what did that mean for him and Lincoln?

Old Lady Carter added, "That's why we wanted to see you off with a good meal and some money in your pocket."

"Oh," Joshua said.

"That corn bread disagree with you?"

"No, ma'am." The price of hoping was being hurt. He knew that. He wondered why he had never quite learned to just quit hoping.

Old Man Carter said, "You need a recommendation anywhere, you tell 'em to ask me. I'll say you work hard."

That was what he had to look forward to: working hard, then moving on, then working hard again. He didn't know if he would ever have a good meal in a clean, warm room again.

He looked at the Carters, who were still smiling at him. They meant well. They didn't have to give him a thing. That made it worse. He wanted to give them their dollar back. He wanted to get up and leave his breakfast behind, half finished. He started to sit back, then heard Lincoln whine at the door, wondering where he was.

He would need all his strength to find a place for Lincoln and himself. Drawing his plate close to his chest, he told the Carters, "I'll tell folks to ask you," then began to eat as fast as he could. He only had the day to find a new place, and he wanted to be out of this one as quickly as he could.

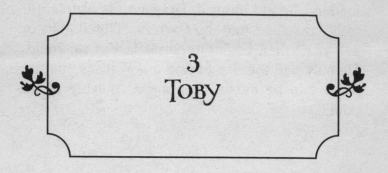

3
TOBY

Toby McGee ran up to the Littleton Shirt Factory. A long line of workers, ranging from girls and boys several years younger than him to women and men old enough to be his great-grandparents, shuffled toward the front gate, where Beasley, the manager, ticked off names on a sheet.

Toby grinned at people as he darted for the end of the line. They called, "Morning, Toby," and "How are you, lad?" and "It's another fine day, wouldn't you say?" He answered, "Morning, Jimmy," and "Fine, Mr. Cassidy," and "It must be if you say so, Mrs. Polansky, for there's no better judge of fine days than you."

That made a smile cross Mrs. Polansky's ancient features. She said, "Ah, you charming Irish rogue."

And that made Toby blush, because Elizabeth O'Leary, half a year older than him and the prettiest girl he had ever seen, put a hand over her mouth to cover a grin after Mrs. Polansky spoke.

Toby got in line behind Mr. Cassidy and a small boy in shabby clothes, probably no older than ten. Toby had never seen the boy before, which made him wonder what work he would do. Then he forgot about the small boy as Nick Finney, a blond boy two months younger than Toby, ran to join him in line. Nick gasped, "Thought I'd never beat the bell."

Toby smiled. "Beasley likes you. If it'd been me—"

"He's a right mean one, that Beasley. You work as hard as anyone, Tobe."

And at three-fourths the pay, Toby thought, but didn't say. The reason for his low pay made him push his right hand deeper into his pocket. He had kept it hidden there since leaving the little room where he lived with his mother, two brothers, and three sisters.

The small boy turned to look shyly at them. Mr. Cassidy glanced back, then jerked his thumb at the boy and said, "This is my son, Danny. He'll be working with you, Nick. Danny, this is Nick Finney and Toby McGee. Toby used to have Nick's job."

Danny's eyes flicked from Toby's face to his

right hand, still in his pocket, and back to his face. Danny asked, "It isn't that hard to do, is it?"

Toby knew what he'd like to say: not hard. Frightening at first, when you're scrambling barefoot up into the cutting machines where adults cannot go, where the long sheets of cloth sometimes get twisted, and it's your job to snatch them free before the machine jams and ruins the cloth in its gears, and all the work in the factory stops until the cloth has been freed and the machine can be started again.

Toby said, "Not if you're careful."

Mr. Cassidy said, "Show 'im what happens if he lets his mind wander."

Toby breathed deeply, then pulled his right hand from his pocket. His mother and Father Andrew had both told him to thank God every day that worse had not happened to him, but looking at his hand, he saw nothing to be thankful for: three fingers missing entirely, the index finger cut above the first joint, only the thumb intact.

Yet that hand let him steady a broom, which gave him a job, which gave his family a roof every night and food most days. Life could be worse. He just didn't know why that should make him grateful.

"You see," Mr. Cassidy told Danny. "You be careful now."

And lucky, Toby thought. Working ten-hour days around dangerous machinery meant you got too tired to be careful all the time. *Pray that God and the Little People look out for you, Danny Cassidy, because you can't always look out for yourself.*

Toby glanced away and caught Elizabeth O'Leary looking back their way. She immediately faced the front of the line. Toby had suspected that she liked Nick. Now his heart sank a bit as he realized it was true. Why else would she be pretending she hadn't looked back at them, if she wasn't checking on Nick?

Then he shrugged. Nick was a good fellow. Liking Nick just meant that she had good taste. Toby might wish that she liked him that way, but if wishing helped, he'd be King Toby the First, and all the lampposts in North America would turn into chocolate.

Nick squinted past Toby. "O'Hara's back."

Toby looked. A small, wiry young man with a shock of red hair walked toward the gate, carrying a sign made out of a stiff sheet of paper tacked to a stick. On it, in neat black letters, was printed WORKERS, UNITE!

Everyone quit talking. O'Hara stopped near the gate and called, "Good morning! Who's ready to join me?"

Mr. Cassidy answered, "Off with you, Pat

O'Hara! Who would join you in not having a job?"

Jimmy Kennedy shouted, "If we strike, they'll just bring in Chinamen to take our place!"

Toby doubted that O'Hara could answer that, because it was true.

Before O'Hara could say anything, Beasley, at the gate, turned his thick spectacles up from his papers, looked at O'Hara, and called over his shoulder, "Johnson! Dupree! Get that man out of here!"

Johnson and Dupree came running from inside the factory. Both of them were taller and heavier than O'Hara. They wore watchmen's uniforms, tailored like police uniforms to suggest that their authority came from the law, not just the company.

Toby didn't want to watch what would happen next. O'Hara had always been kind to him. When Toby's money had run out before payday because one of his brothers needed medicine, O'Hara had given him half of his lunch.

But two days ago, O'Hara had said that if they all refused to work until Littleton made changes, he would have to raise their pay, shorten their workday from ten hours to eight, and make their working conditions safer. When Beasley had heard about it, he had fired O'Hara on the spot. Everyone said that O'Hara was an idealistic fool. No one had thought he would ever come back.

Johnson told O'Hara, "You're not wanted here."

"No," O'Hara agreed. "But I'm needed."

"Get," said Dupree.

"The sidewalk's public," said O'Hara. "You've no right to send me away."

Dupree and Johnson looked at Beasley. Beasley said, "You're obstructing traffic, O'Hara."

"Obstructing traffic," Dupree repeated.

"All by my own self?" O'Hara said with a smile, holding his arms wide to indicate how small a crowd he made.

Elizabeth O'Leary laughed, and Toby grinned. Beasley turned quickly to see who might be on O'Hara's side, but Elizabeth frowned, and Nick elbowed Toby, which made him grimace. It was one thing to admire O'Hara. It was another to lose your job because of it.

"He won't go," Johnson told Beasley.

O'Hara called to the line, "If the bosses won't improve working conditions, we have to make them! Look at Toby if you think I'm wrong!"

Toby looked at the sidewalk and pushed his hand even deeper into his pocket. Everyone's gaze burned him like fire. Elizabeth's was like the heat at the heart of the sun. He thought, *Sod O'Hara, anyway. He's just making a show of himself from pride.*

Beasley said, "O'Hara, will you leave peace-fully?"

"Sure, I will," said O'Hara. "When I've fin-ished my business here."

Beasley turned to Johnson and Dupree. "Do I have to tell you how to do your work?"

"No, sir," said Johnson, and he hit O'Hara in the face.

O'Hara fell hard onto the cobblestone street. Blood spurted from his nose. Toby closed his eyes, seeing his own blood flowing from his hand—

Then he bumped into Mr. Cassidy and opened his eyes. The line had come to a stop. Toby saw Johnson step on O'Hara's sign. Its wooden handle cracked under his boot, sounding like a rifle shot in the silence.

Mr. Cassidy started forward, making a fist. Mrs. Polansky caught his arm, indicated Danny, and whispered, "You've got children to feed, Mick!" Mr. Cassidy slumped as if the air had been let out of him. Then the work bell rang out, reminding Toby why he was there.

O'Hara sat up in the street and wiped blood from his nose with the back of his hand. "Join me!" he shouted. "Together, we're strong!"

No one moved, not toward O'Hara or the gate. Toby looked away because he couldn't bear to meet O'Hara's eyes.

Beasley broke the long moment of silence by calling, "Anyone who wants to work today, come along. Anyone who doesn't is welcome to stay outside."

Nick whispered, "It's not right."

Toby's hand throbbed in his pocket. He said the same words his mother had spoken so many times: "Plenty happens that isn't right. You have to live with it, that's all."

From the corner of his eye, he could see Nick giving him a curious look, but Toby didn't feel like meeting his eyes or talking.

The line began to move again. No one spoke. Toby kept his gaze on the ground. Maybe he should have done something, but then he thought of his mother and the little ones needing food and rent and told himself he'd done right in doing nothing. Better to put up with this than let a Chinaman take his place and have everyone he loved thrown out on the street.

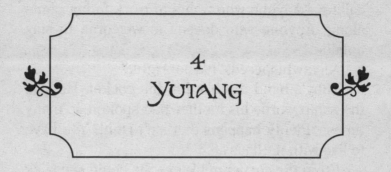

4
YUTANG

Lin Yutang walked away from his family's furniture repair shop. Across his shoulders lay a long pole with six wooden chairs hanging from it, three on either side of him. Yutang walked in the street because the pole and the chairs were too wide for the sidewalk. Whenever he saw a carriage, a cart, a wagon, or a trolley approaching, he had to turn sideways to let the vehicle pass, but he did not mind that. The six chairs were heavy, but he did not mind that, either. He felt light, and with each step away from home, he felt lighter.

He knew he should be afraid as he left the safety of San Francisco's Chinatown, where he understood the people and the language, and entered the city of the round-eyed barbarians. But in Chinatown, he was always aware that he must be a good son to his parents. When he became a man, they expected him to go to China and find a wife. That idea made them smile, but Yutang always hid his face whenever it was mentioned. China was their home, not his.

Sometimes he felt as if he lived in a cage, like his family's pet cricket and pet songbird. Their cages were made of bamboo; Yutang's was made of virtue. Sometimes he dreamed of running away and becoming a pirate king, the most powerful pirate king who had ever lived—

He was so deep in his thoughts that he did not immediately recognize a barbarian's voice calling, "Yutang! Lin Yutang!" in a British accent. But the call made him stop in the street and look back over his shoulder.

A dark-bearded barbarian wearing an admiral's blue uniform bedecked with medals walked quickly toward him. The man's eyes were wild, as always, but also kind, as always. Yutang turned sideways, set his pole and the six heavy chairs down along the side of the road so they would not block traffic, and bowed deeply.

"Your Majesty," Yutang said in English. "How are you today?"

"Very well, very well," the man replied, seeming pleased and impatient and distracted all at once. Almost everyone in San Francisco knew Emperor Norton the First, the self-proclaimed

Emperor of the United States and Protector of Mexico. When he needed to buy something, he gave out banknotes that he had printed up, drawn on a treasury that existed only in his mind. Most people accepted his notes as if they were real money, because he was kind and amusing. He had always traveled with his most faithful subjects, two dogs named Lazarus and Bummer. When Lazarus had died, ten thousand people had gone to his funeral.

Bummer ran up to lick Yutang's hands and sniff his feet. While Yutang patted the dog, Emperor Norton asked, "How are my faithful subjects from the Celestial Empire?"

"There is no trouble in Chinatown, Your Majesty."

"I am pleased. Very pleased. Distressing news from Los Angeles. Very distressing."

A mob of white Americans, angry at being out of work, had killed nineteen Chinese settlers, claiming that the Chinese were stealing work from them. "Yes, Your Majesty," Yutang answered. "It is much better here."

"Good. Glad to hear it. Something must be done. Can't believe something like that could happen under my rule. I'll issue a decree. Won't happen again."

"I hope you're right, Your Majesty."

Most Chinese in San Francisco respected the

emperor. One day, angry barbarians had gathered to attack Chinatown. Norton had come and placed himself in front of them, where he had loudly recited the Lord's Prayer. Ashamed of themselves, the people in the mob had wandered away, leaving Chinatown alone.

So Yutang waited patiently while Emperor Norton nodded to himself. Yutang wondered if he was about to be dismissed, but Norton said abruptly, "Your English is very good, Lin Yutang."

"Thank you, Your Majesty."

"It could be better."

"Yes, Your Majesty."

"There's a minister starting a school for Celestials. School's a good thing, eh? You read English?"

"Some." He knew enough to make a list of furniture for his customers.

"Good, good." The emperor patted the pockets of his uniform until he came up with a pencil stub and a banknote. "Money may be the root of all evil, but the paper sort has many uses." Norton scribbled an address and the name of a barbarian on the banknote and handed it to Yutang. "See if the teacher has room for you. Then spend that on something nice."

"Thank you, Your Majesty." The banknote was worthless, and Yutang had already visited the barbarian teacher, only to find that there would be no room for new students for years. Yutang bowed, folded the note carefully, and slipped it into his pocket.

Norton waved his hand. "Never pass up a chance to make the world a better place."

"Yes, Your Majesty."

Yutang smiled as he watched the emperor and Bummer walk on. Norton acknowledged each person he passed with a gracious greeting, and Bummer gave them all a quick sniff before he raced to catch up to the first Emperor of the United States of America. Then Yutang shouldered the pole supporting the six chairs and walked on.

He had not been walking for five minutes when he saw two barbarian men in suits talking in front of a tavern. One looked his way and muttered something loudly about the "heathen Chinee." The other glanced toward him. This barbarian wore a shiny star pinned to his dark suit.

Yutang dropped his gaze to the ground and kept walking. His breathing sped up. He told himself that he had done nothing wrong, but then, what had the nineteen Chinese in Los Angeles done to make the barbarians hate them?

The policeman called, "Boy! Chinaboy! Over here!"

Yutang nodded and trotted up the street as

quickly as he could. When he reached the tavern, he stopped as he had before, carefully turning the pole and chairs and setting them down so they would not be in anyone's way.

The policeman said, "Speakee English, Chinaboy?"

Yutang dipped his head politely. "Yes, sir."

"Then I reckon you ain't got no excuse."

"Excuse for what, sir?"

The policeman turned to his companion. "They never admit nothing."

"Slippery devils," the other barbarian agreed. "What do you expect? They don't have Christian morals."

The policeman sighed. "Ain't it the truth?" He glanced at Yutang. "There's a law against carrying things on a pole in San Francisco. Them things block traffic."

Yutang stared at the policeman, then at the chairs, then bowed to the policeman. "Sir, I did not know—"

"Well, now you do."

"Yes, sir."

"What're you going to do about it?"

"Sir?"

"I said, what're you going to do about it?"

He answered quickly, "I will not carry anything on a pole in San Francisco."

The policeman laughed and nudged the other

man. "This one speaks pretty good, don't he?"

"Makes him trickier," said the other man.

"So why aren't you slipping that pole out from them chairs?" asked the policeman.

"Please, sir. I must deliver them—"

The policeman shrugged. "Ain't my problem, boy. That's yours."

"Yes, sir." Yutang looked around, knowing that sometimes help would come in time of need. But there were no other Chinese nearby to aid him.

"Something holding you up?" asked the policeman. Before, his voice had been amused, which was dangerous enough, but now it had a frightening edge.

"No, sir," Yutang answered. "But please, sir, may I carry these chairs to the Seamen's Hotel? It is not far."

"What did I tell you?"

"That there is a law—"

"That's right. And it's my job to uphold that law."

"Yes, sir."

"You want me to fine you for breaking that law?"

"No, sir."

"You know I'm doing you a favor, don't you, boy?"

"Yes, sir," Yutang lied. The Pirate King would

have lost patience and beheaded this barbarian, and his smiling friend too, with a single sweep of his long, sharp sword.

"So what're you going to do?"

"I shall remove the pole."

The policeman nodded. "And I reckon you might throw it away, so you won't be tempted to use it again."

"There's a firewood pile alongside the tavern," said the other man.

The policeman held out his hand.

Yutang looked at the chairs and the pole. The pole was sturdy, and comfortable on his shoulders. His people had carried loads on poles for centuries. But the barbarians did not use poles, so they had now forbidden others to use them. That seemed to be the way of barbarians.

Yutang pulled out the pole and handed it to the policeman. The man took one end in both hands, put the other end against the ground, and stamped on it with his foot. The pole broke with a loud, crisp *crack*.

"That'll make fine kindling." The policeman handed the two pieces of the pole back to Yutang. "Now it won't be a temptation to you. Go throw that away, boy."

Yutang took the broken pole as the other man laughed. The Pirate King would have them tied to a stake and set on fire. Or maybe he would bury them in the sand at low tide where they could watch the waves coming up to drown them. Or maybe—

"Yes, sir," Yutang said. He ran around the side of the building, threw the pieces of his pole onto a woodpile, and ran back, afraid that something would have happened to the chairs while he was gone. But the two barbarians still stood there, laughing together, and the chairs had not been touched.

"Well, then," the policeman said. "I figure I can teach you something about America."

You have already taught me something about America, Yutang thought, letting his face show nothing.

"What do you say when someone does you a favor?" asked the policeman.

"Thank you, sir," said Yutang.

"That's right." The policeman pointed at the six chairs. "Now get them out of here, or I'll have to charge you for dumping trash in the street."

"But, sir—"

The policeman's eyes narrowed.

Yutang stopped his protest. "Thank you, sir."

The policeman smiled. "All right, then. See they're gone by the time I come out." The policeman nudged his friend, and they laughed and went inside the tavern.

Yutang stared at the six chairs. If he tried to

stack them on top of each other to carry them, the finish would be scratched, and the customer would be furious. If he put them back to back, he could only carry two with one hand and two with the other. If he put one upside down on the other, so they rested with their seats together, he would be no better off. He could balance a fifth one upside down on his head, but the sixth would have to be kicked along in front of him, and if he did that, it would be damaged as surely as if he had stacked it.

He wanted to cry, but he would never do that in front of barbarians. He wanted to hurt someone, but Buddha taught that when you hurt others, you hurt yourself.

He breathed deeply to calm himself. His father would say that there are always answers to be found if you look long enough. His mother would say that sometimes you overlook an answer because it is not as easy as you would like, but an answer is still an answer.

He turned one chair upside down and put it onto another one, so the one on top had its legs sticking up into the air. Then he set a third chair on that with its legs pointing down, so the feet rested on the underside of the seat of the chair beneath it. For a second, he considered building a tower that way, but it would be too tall and unsteady to carry safely.

So he made a second stack of three chairs like the other one. Then he picked that one up and carried it a quarter of a block down the street. He set it down and ran back to the first stack, carrying it as quickly as he could up to the first stack and a quarter of a block farther. Then he put that one down and ran back for the first. It was as if he were playing leapfrog with himself. By repeating the process over and over, he would end up walking twice as far and taking twice as long as he would have if the policeman had let him carry all the chairs on the pole. But he knew that he would get the chairs to their owner eventually. So he tried not to think about how it could have been easier if things were different. He just kept going back and forth, moving each stack of chairs farther than the one he had moved before.

The plan worked fine for the first mile. He passed a dark-skinned barbarian boy who offered to help for a dime, but Yutang had no money to spare, so he turned the barbarian down and kept going.

Most people walked by Yutang and stared at him. Some of them laughed, but if that was the price of getting the job done, he would pay it. Barbarians were like monkeys, amused by things that they did not understand.

But when he was into the second mile, he ran back for one stack of chairs only to find a young barbarian man in rough clothing standing beside it. The man was tall and thin, with pale hair, pimples, and a fuzzy lip that looked like a caterpillar had died on it. The man grinned, and Yutang knew his troubles were far from over.

The man said, "You're too late, John Chinaman."

Yutang did not want to ask, but he could see no way to avoid it. "Too late for what, please, sir?"

"I found these here chairs first."

"Please. I must deliver them."

"Well, now, I must too, now that I found them. You volunteering to help carry 'em into my place?"

"No, sir. Please. Let me take them."

"Why should I do that?" The man smiled. He had lost two of his front teeth.

"Because it is my job, sir."

"Well. All right, then," said the man. "I suppose you can take them. It's only Christian."

For a moment, Yutang thought that the man was content with a bit of teasing. Often people— especially barbarians—made fun of him, got bored, and let him go on with whatever he was doing. Then the man with the fuzzy lip said, "There's another pile o' chairs just up the block. You can have these, an' I'll take the others."

Yutang screwed up his courage. "Please, sir. I must take those, too."

The man blinked at him. "My, you are a greedy one, ain't you? I reckon that's the Chinee for you. Always a-grabbin' all they can get."

"Please, sir," Yutang said. "Their owner will want the chairs."

"Then he shouldn'ta left 'em in the street, I figure," said the man, giving his gap-toothed smile again. "On second thought, I'll take these. Won't have to carry them as far as if I took the others, right?"

Yutang stared at him.

The man frowned. "Best get a move on, Chinaboy. Someone's going to claim them other chairs if you're not careful. What'll you have, then?"

Yutang closed his fists tight at his sides.

The man laughed. "You fixing to fight me, Chinaboy?"

And what would Yutang gain if he did? The man was taller and heavier. If they created a disturbance and the police came, barbarian law would side with the barbarian—it always did. Yutang relaxed his hands.

"Didn't think so," said the man.

"I will carry these away now," Yutang suggested.

"I told you. Finders keepers. Now get."

If he let the man take the chairs, their owner would demand payment, and his father's honor would require that the payment be made immediately. His parents might be forced to sell their store. And then his mother and father would have to start over again, with nothing but the worthless son who was responsible for their misfortune.

As the barbarian reached for the chairs, Yutang knew that only bad answers were available to him. Without the slightest idea which one he would choose, he stepped between the man and the chairs.

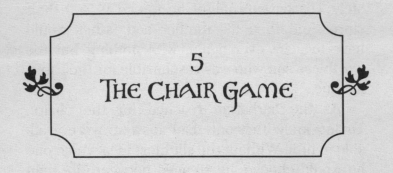

5
THE CHAIR GAME

Joshua and Lincoln walked the streets of San Francisco without a destination. To be more precise, Joshua walked without a destination—Joshua himself was the big dog's destination. Wherever he led, Lincoln followed, ambling contentedly by his master's side.

Joshua knocked at each door that he came to, saying, "Excuse me, sir" or "Excuse me, ma'am," and "I'm looking for some work. I'm handy, and I work hard." Sometimes doors were slammed in his face before he had finished his short speech. Most of the time, with varying degrees of politeness, he heard "no." A few times, he was told where he might find work, but when he went to those places, he discovered that "no" had merely been postponed. Perhaps the most honest answer came from an Irish housemaid who laughed and said, "Grown white men are desperate for any work they can get. Who's going to hire a black boy?"

After a long morning of rejections, Joshua sat on a street curb. Lincoln came and laid his heavy head on Joshua's thigh.

Joshua lifted a bottle of water from his coat pocket, took a long drink of cool water, then poured some in his palm for Lincoln to lap up. As the hound drank, Joshua said, "Getting tired, old boy?"

Lincoln looked up at him, then started drinking again.

"Me too." Joshua smiled. "Well, we'll just go until we find something better. What do you think?"

Lincoln fixed his big brown eyes on Joshua in solemn agreement.

As he sat there, an Asian boy, with his hair in a pigtail down to his waist and wearing a loose, dark Chinese jacket and trousers, carried a stack of three chairs around the corner and past him, heading down toward the sea. The boy set the chairs down halfway up the block, then ran back past Joshua, went around the corner, and reappeared with a second stack of three chairs. As the boy came by Joshua for the third time,

Joshua said, "You got far to carry those?"

"Yes, sir," said the boy. "To the Seamen's Hotel."

Joshua smiled. He had never been called "sir" before in his life. "I can help you," he said. "For ten cents."

The boy shook his head. "Thank you, sir. But I can carry them."

Joshua nodded sadly. "You do that," he said. If he hadn't had the Carters' dollar in his pocket, he would have counteroffered to help for a nickel. It was nice to have the luxury of being able to let a job go, even if it was a very little job that would not have changed his life for the better.

He watched the Chinese boy move the two stacks of chairs down the street. It seemed like a silly way to do a job. A sensible person would've gotten a wagon or carried one stack of chairs to their destination, then gone back for the other. But then, the boy dressed funny and talked funny and wasn't Christian. Why expect him to behave sensibly?

Lincoln settled his head in Joshua's lap.

"Well, all right," Joshua agreed. "We'll rest a minute more." He stroked the old dog's head.

As he sat there, he began to think about impossible things, like finding a school that would teach poor black students. A minister had taught him to read, so now he read any scrap of

writing he came across. That only made him realize how much more he could learn, if he could
only have the chance.

But his grandmother had said that wishing
won't fill washtubs. "Let's go," he announced as
he stood.

Joshua and Lincoln had only gone a few
blocks when Lincoln suddenly turned down a
street leading toward the sea. Joshua said,
"Come on, boy, I was thinking we would see if
there was work around the train station first—"
Then Joshua heard someone laugh.

A mustached white man faced the Chinese
boy by one stack of chairs. The second stack of
chairs was farther down the street.

"I will carry these away now," the boy
offered.

"I told you," the white man said. "Finders
keepers. Now get."

The boy stepped between the man and the
chairs. "Sir, they are not yours."

The man pushed the boy away, and the boy
stumbled. "They are now."

"They aren't," Joshua said.

The man and the Chinese boy both stared at
him. Joshua told himself that he shouldn't have
gotten into this without knowing what was going
on. Then he realized that he did know what was
going on. The white man was taking the Chinese

boy's chairs because he thought that he could get away with it. And if Joshua didn't say anything, the man would be right.

The man said, "Them your chairs?"

"No. Not yours, either."

"You're mighty sure of yourself."

"I saw him carry those chairs down the street," Joshua stated. "I don't know if they're his, but they're sure not yours." He glanced at the boy. "They belong to the Seaman's Hotel?"

"Yes," said the boy.

"They belong to me now," said the man. He raised his fist. "If you're smart—"

Lincoln growled. Joshua caught the gray dog by the scruff and explained, "Sometimes he gets this notion folks are threatening me, and he goes all wild."

The man took a step back. "I never threatened you."

"Oh, sure, I know that. But you have to tell Lincoln."

"Excuse me?"

"That's the dog."

"I'm not explaining one thing to a dog!"

Lincoln growled again. The white man's face grew whiter.

Joshua said, "He hears your voice, and it sounds to him like you're mad. He's just a dog. He doesn't know much."

"I'm not explaining to a stupid mutt!" the man repeated, backing into the house and slamming the door.

Joshua said, "Huh. Guess he decided those weren't his chairs, after all."

The Chinese boy said, "I will give you a dime."

"What for?"

"Helping me carry the chairs down to the wharf."

"Well," said Joshua, "all right." He slid his bag of possessions around to his back, picked up the stack of chairs, and told Lincoln, "You are the most unfriendly dog I ever met. I don't know why I keep you around."

Lincoln brushed his side against Joshua's faded trousers. "Oh, all right. I guess I do," Joshua agreed before Lincoln could push him over, and he headed down the street to catch up to the Chinese boy.

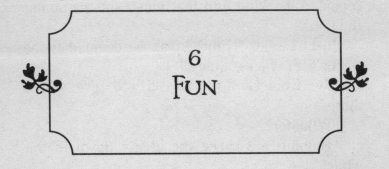

6
FUN

At the top of Nob Hill, overlooking the city and the bay, Toby waited in front of the Littleton mansion. A cool winter breeze rolled over him, and the air smelled of grass and pine trees. Everything about the house and lawn was as perfect as could be. The house was painted a bright yellow with white, blue, and green trim. The trees, bushes, and grass were neatly clipped. The stone walkway was so clean and white that it might have just been placed that morning, and the circular carriage drive looked as if it had been stolen from a palace—which, in a sense, it had. The maid who had briefed Toby on how to behave had said, "Mrs. Littleton simply pointed at one of her paintings and told the architect, 'I want *that*.' Imagine! You want something, you say

so, and it's yours. Wouldn't that be grand?" And
Toby had agreed that that would be grand.

He thought that he should be feeling grand
himself, being paid to be outdoors on a beautiful
day during the week. But he knew that one thing
was glaringly wrong with this scene of expensive
comfort, and he was it: a dirty redheaded boy in
a battered cap and an oversized coat standing by
the pristine drive.

All Toby needed to do, according to Beasley,
was fetch a package for the Littletons. They
needed someone because half of their servants
were in bed with the flu, and Mrs. Littleton was
not the sort to wait when a brand-new dress from
Paris had just arrived by steamship.

A beautiful older woman in swathes of white
cloth like an angel came down the front steps, followed by the maid who had instructed Toby. He
kept his right hand in his pocket. With his left, he
tugged at his cap. "Morning, ma'am," he said,
certain that every word he spoke sounded wrong
in this place.

The angel—Mrs. Littleton—wrinkled her
nose slightly as she studied him. He wanted to
tell her something that he had heard O'Hara say,
that he was grimy with her dirt because his work
in the factory helped her live in her clean, beautiful home.

Mrs. Littleton handed him a folded slip of paper. "Give this to the purser of the *Rosamund*. He'll give you my package."

"Yes, ma'am."

She held out her hand again. "And here are two nickels for the streetcars. It's a rather long walk."

Toby took the coins and grinned at the idea of being paid to ride through the city. "Thank you, ma'am."

Mrs. Littleton smiled. "I can't bear to wait an instant longer than necessary for my dress. I'm sure your mother's the same way."

His mother only owned two dresses, and she had sewn them both herself, but Toby knew Mrs. Littleton didn't want to hear about that. He nodded. "Yes, ma'am. I won't dawdle."

"Good boy." She turned back toward the house.

Realizing he had been dismissed, Toby turned on his heel and walked quickly away. He did not slow down, not as he strode down the front path, nor when he turned onto the driveway, nor when he reached the main gate. Only when he came to the front sidewalk did he pause to look back at the beautiful woman in her beautiful clothes going into her beautiful house. He thought of his mother washing clothes by the river to earn a few pennies, then squeezed his maimed right hand into a fist and hurried away.

Walking to the cable car stop, he passed several people dressed in expensive clothes. When a young man frowned at the dirty boy in the wealthy neighborhood, Toby merely walked faster. But when a middle-aged man and woman did the same thing, Toby pulled his right hand from his pocket and touched it to his cap. And he took cold satisfaction from seeing them wince and look away.

When he came to the cable car stop, he decided to walk a little farther, then halted and scuffed his feet as though he had to clean the soles of his shoes. A car moved toward him, pulled along by the thick wire cable in a channel running down the street. Only a few passengers sat along the car's side.

Toby started walking downhill on the sidewalk, following the cable car track. The driver released the car from the cable and braked to a stop, letting off two young ladies carrying bright hatboxes. Then he threw the lever to clamp the car back onto the cable. It pulled forward, coming up beside Toby.

He angled across the street as if he were going to the other side. He slowed to let the cable car go by. The driver, a young man with a large black mustache, waved. Toby waved back.

As the car passed, he jumped and caught onto

its back, first with his left hand, then steadying himself with what was left of his right. He found toeholds as the car picked up speed. *There's five more cents for the family,* he thought. *Wish every five cents I made was this much fun.* Boys had fallen from the backs of the cars and hurt themselves, but he had a good grip. He smiled all the way down the steep hill.

The car passed another climbing upward. A well-dressed woman glanced at Toby, then looked back to stare. He tipped his cap to her. The woman's eyes opened wide, and she shook her head from side to side to show her disapproval. Toby bit his lip to keep from laughing so loudly that the driver would hear and throw him off.

At the bottom of the hill, an elderly man with thin white hair got onto the back of the car, then noticed Toby and glared at him. "You're stealing a ride. You're no better than a thief."

"Please, sir," Toby said. "Don't say anything."

"Driver!" the old man shouted.

Toby dropped lightly onto the street. He waved his cap to the old man in the cable car and called, "Have a nice trip, sir!"

He walked across the city, thinking about luck. His mother and father had both told him there wasn't much of it in Ireland, where the

English ruled cruelly and over a million people had starved to death during the great famines. But where was the luck in America, where his father had been crushed by a runaway wagon and Toby had lost half of his hand?

When the air grew thick with the smell of the sea, and the dunes became visible, and the horizon was interrupted by ships' masts instead of buildings, Toby saw a wheelbarrow full of gravel where workmen had left it. He snatched a handful and dropped it into his pocket. Somewhere, the perfect target—a bottle on a post, a broken window in an abandoned house, or something even better than those—was waiting for him.

At the wharf, he stared in awe at the ships and the bustle of passengers and visitors and workers as people and goods moved back and forth. He found the clipper ship *Rosamund* and started to ask for its purser. Then he realized that as soon as he did, his adventure would be over.

He looked out at the bay. A modern ship steamed into the harbor as the sails of a four-masted ship filled, carrying it toward some exotic port. *I'd like to be a sailor someday,* he thought. *Maybe a captain.* He smiled, then remembered his hand. Who would hire a crippled sailor?

It was time to get Mrs. Littleton's package and return, but Toby hesitated. He took a last look at all the ships in the bay and inhaled deeply, filling his lungs with the smells of salt and fish.

His mother would be amazed when he told her where he'd been. She'd never been down to the wharf. She always had to look after the little ones. Maybe he would bring the family down one Sunday afternoon. He smiled, thinking how they would like that. He watched a tiny boy chase a seagull and imagined little Meg laughing at it. He would like to come here with Nick sometime, and maybe they could invite Elizabeth O'Leary—

Toby heard a bark somewhere in the crowds of workers and passengers. He looked closer. Just past a black boy and a big gray dog, a Chinese boy with black pajamas and a pigtail walked alone on the wharf.

Staring at the Chinese boy, Toby saw the simple answer to the questions that troubled him. Jimmy Kennedy had said the Chinese stole work from Americans by working for cheap wages. Toby saw the small room that his family rented while the Littletons lived in a mansion. He saw his mother sweating by the river, washing other people's clothes, while Mrs. Littleton went to parties. He saw his father lying in a rough wooden casket while Mr. Littleton counted the money from his factories. He saw the cutting machine where he had worked all day to try to make things better for his mother and brothers and sisters, and then he saw his own blood—

Toby reached into his pocket and drew out a small rock. It fit perfectly between his thumb and the stump of his index finger.

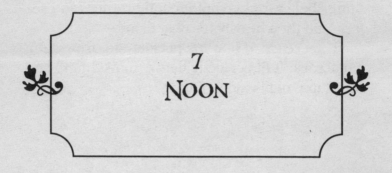

7

NOON

This was the Pirate King's air, Yutang thought as he breathed in deeply. This was his place, where the gulls cried to each other, and the winds scoured the beach, and ships rocked upon the waves, and people hurried along the wharves, moving goods and planning to travel to places where no one mocked them.

"It's awful pretty," said the dark barbarian by his side.

That spoiled the moment. Yutang did not know the word in English to describe what the Pirate King saw. Not beauty. Power, maybe, or possibility.

Yutang said, "Thank you for your help. Here is your dime."

The barbarian took the coin and slipped it

into his pocket. "Thanks." But instead of leaving, he asked, "What's your name?"

"Lin Yutang."

"I'm Joshua Green, from Alabama."

"I am from China."

"You don't say." Joshua grinned. "I had a couple of clues. Why do you wear those pajamas, anyway?"

When barbarians became amused, Chinese people were wise to worry. But Yutang did not wish to be rude, not even to a poor dark barbarian. They, after all, were despised by many of the light-skinned ones. He had to feel pity for the boy, and gratitude for his assistance with the chairs.

"My clothes," Yutang explained, "are more comfortable than the clothes of westerners. My hair is in a queue to show respect to the Emperor of China."

"You aren't in China now."

And Yutang had never been in China, he admitted silently. "It is our custom."

"I've seen Chinamen who don't have queues."

Yutang sighed. "Some westerners cut our queues to amuse themselves. There's a law that prisoners must have short hair—some Chinese are arrested for things they did not do or did not understand, and their heads are shaved. And some of our people cut their hair to be like Americans."

"Does that work?"

"I do not think so."

"That's why you don't cut your hair?"

Yutang saw nothing cruel in the barbarian's smile, so he said, "I shall return to China when I am a man. My father does not wish for me to forget that."

"Your father fixes furniture?"

"My mother and I help him."

"He need any help? I'm looking for work. And a place to stay."

Yutang almost laughed at the idea of bringing a barbarian and a dog into their shop, but Joshua seemed very serious, so he only answered, "I am afraid not."

"Well, I had to ask. Good luck, Lin Yutang."

"And to you, Joshua Green." Yutang nodded in farewell, turned away, and walked out onto the wharf. From behind him, he heard Joshua call, "Lincoln! No matter how much you water that post, it won't grow. Let's get a move on."

Yutang smiled as he continued up the wharf, carefully staying out of everyone's way. A donkey pulling a cart filled with fish passed him. He saw one of the fish flip itself, and he thought, *I'm sorry, Fish. May you be born into a better life next time.*

Someone shouted, "Lin Yutang! Duck!" He turned. Something flashed in the sunlight, heading toward his face. He twisted sideways as a small stone hit the side of his head.

A second stone hit him in the shoulder. Gasping as much in surprise as pain, he saw who had thrown them: a red-haired barbarian boy whose clothes looked little better than Joshua's.

Yutang ducked as the redhead threw more pebbles. Around them, some barbarians ignored his trouble. Some looked with disapproval at the redhead, but said nothing. Some grinned, enjoying the show. Yutang thought he saw Joshua walking away, passing behind a stack of crates. Then a stone hit Yutang's ear, and he forgot about Joshua.

Dodging the redhead's barrage, Yutang ran along the wharf, came to the end, and turned back. He was trapped. The only way off was to pass the redhead. No, there was a second way. He glanced down at the waves.

In the rigging of a nearby ship, a pale barbarian sailor called, "Better swim for it, John Chinaman!"

"Don't stop till you get to China!" shouted a dark barbarian porter moving a crate.

The Pirate King would dive and swim away, planning to return to take his revenge. But Yutang could not swim. He scrambled along the end of the wharf, wishing for cover and trying to protect his face with his arms. The redhead yelled, "Dance, you Chinese ape!"

Yutang wanted to drop where he was and cover his head. But if he did, his attacker might come closer. He had to escape.

He darted to his right. As stones flew toward him, he cut left. The redhead was taller and heavier than Yutang; if the boy grabbed him, he would be trapped. But with enough speed and luck, he would slip by. Hoping he had both, he ran as hard as he could.

Then he heard Joshua shout, "Leave him alone!"

The rain of stones slackened as the redhead turned to stare at Joshua. Yutang burst past both boys. In three steps, he thought he had made it, and in five, he knew he had. The crowd of white and black faces parted for him. A man clapped him on the shoulder, saying, "Good running, John Chinaman!"

Yutang glanced back as the redhead tackled Joshua. The boys rolled across the wooden planks of the wharf, the big gray dog barking and circling them.

Around the fighters, the crowd was growing. Someone yelled, "Show him who's boss!"

Yutang stared at the scene. The redhead was

larger than Joshua; he was clearly winning. Yutang had paid Joshua for his work. He owed him nothing. He should head as quickly as possible for Chinatown, where he knew the dangers and how to find safety. Why, then, was he running directly at the redhead and screaming at the top of his lungs?

Yutang threw himself onto the redhead, who kept his hold on Joshua. The three boys rolled across the rough boards. Then Yutang was in some space where there was no up or down, only emptiness. The sky rushed toward them, but the sky looked like rolling waves. They were falling.

All he had wanted was to stop the fight. He'd never wanted them all to drown. He hoped that would be taken into account when it was time to be reborn into a better life or a worse one.

Hitting the water was like hitting glass that instantly dissolved beneath him. The cold ocean closed over him. He thrashed desperately, and his head broke into the air. Gulping half air and half seawater, he gasped, "Help!" and sank again.

His lungs burned. He could see nothing. He fought the water for long seconds, until he realized that the water was going to win. That made him struggle harder.

He wondered if his parents would think he had run away. He wished he could tell everyone that he was sorry for anything he had done that had hurt them, and he wondered whether he would enter his next life as a fish.

Something jerked his long braid. He flailed about in the frigid darkness, hitting nothing, then saw that the water was growing brighter. Whatever had him was drawing him up toward the air, away from his next life, back toward the one that he did not want to leave.

He burst into the sunlight. A dark head bobbed in the water like a melon. Yutang clutched for it. When something struck his chest to push him back, he saw that the head was Joshua Green's, and that the dark barbarian was holding him away at arm's length.

"It's okay!" Joshua shouted. "Grab onto Lincoln! Try to float on your back!"

Yutang saw the dog paddling beside them. He caught onto the dog's rough coat and thought, *I must be calm.* He had heard about drowning people who clutched desperately onto the people trying to rescue them, causing them both to drown. But it was hard to be calm with the waves tossing them and the water hungry to swallow him.

"Help!" someone called as Yutang tried to lie on his back. A wave lifted him. For a moment, he could see the redhead drifting away from the wharf, caught by the current. Then the pale barbarian went under.

"That boy!" Yutang shouted, pointing and getting a mouthful of saltwater for his effort.

"I see him!" Joshua swam away, leaving Yutang with Lincoln.

Joshua dove where the redhead had gone under. For a long moment, Yutang wondered if Joshua would ever come up again. He did not realize that he had been holding his breath in sympathy until he gasped air. A second later, Joshua surfaced, pulling the boy after him.

Above them, the crowd cheered, then grew silent. Yutang lifted his head. He saw the redhead spitting water and Joshua staring past him in amazement.

A new wave lifted Yutang and Lincoln. He saw what Joshua and the crowd saw and, for an instant, he forgot that they were all still in danger of drowning.

A boat raced toward them. The blades of its oars flashed in the sunlight as the rowers drove them through the water. From the bow, someone called, "Hold on! We'll get you out!"

Yutang blinked twice, wondering whether he had drowned after all and this was a hallucination.

The boat was tiny and painted in rich burgundy and gold. Two tiny, pale barbarians in bright red coats and tall black hats pulled its oars, one tiny man to an oar. At the bow sat a blond man with a goatee. He wore a brown business suit, which ought to have meant he looked rather ordinary. But though he was a giant beside the tiny men in red coats, he was no taller than a four-year-old boy.

They were being rescued by circus midgets.

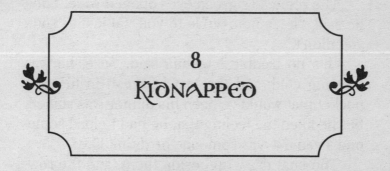

8
KIDNAPPED

Paddling to keep himself and the redheaded boy afloat, Joshua stared at the boat, the small blond man in its bow, and the even smaller rowers in their red coats and stovepipe hats. Just beyond them, tied to the wharf, lay a little ship that looked as if it had sailed out of a painting of Columbus finding America. He had seen that ship every time he had looked at the bay, he realized, but every time his eyes had slid over it as if it weren't there. Now he saw it clearly. It was like waking from a dream, or waking *into* one.

But this wasn't the time to wonder about ships. He jerked his head to check on Lincoln and saw the big gray dog pulling Yutang easily through the waves. Joshua glanced back at the redhead, who spat water and said, "I never asked you to save me."

"I can let go," Joshua suggested.

The redhead's green eyes opened wide. Then he said, "If it's no trouble to you, I'd just as soon you didn't."

"It's no trouble," Joshua said. Sure, he was freezing cold, and the loaf of bread in his coat pocket that would've been his dinner was ruined, but he liked the feeling that he had helped someone, even if it was someone he didn't like.

The boat drew up beside them, and the rowers extended their oars. "Catch on to 'em!" the blond man called. He looked like a banker or a lawyer in his brown suit and his vest printed with orange flowers. His blond hair was combed back from his forehead. His mustache and goatee gave him a slightly wild, slightly dangerous look, like a gambler or a cavalry officer.

The boys caught the oars and scrambled into the boat with the little men's help. Joshua saw the redhead's right hand clearly for the first time as the boy used his thumb and maimed finger like a lobster's claw to grip first an oar, then the side of the boat. For an instant, Joshua felt pity for the boy. Then he remembered the accuracy of the stones he had thrown, and how hard he had been able to hit with both his good hand and his maimed one.

The redhead saw him looking and pushed his hand into his pocket. Joshua turned away to grab

Lincoln's front paws and pull the heavy dog into the boat.

The redhead took a bench by the rowers. Yutang sat at the stern. Shivering, Joshua huddled beside Yutang. Lincoln shook himself, spraying all the boys with water, then lay across Joshua and Yutang's feet.

The blond man grinned at the sodden boys. "Quite a catch," he said, and the rowers laughed as they started toward the ship. Joshua scratched Lincoln's head, then glanced up at the wharf. Now that the boys were safe, the crowd had left.

The redhead looked back at Joshua. He mumbled, "Wanted to say"—he swallowed, then finished—"thanks. My name's Toby."

Joshua shook his head. "You got nothing to thank me for."

"Well, and isn't my life something?"

"My life, too," said Yutang. "I thank you, Joshua Green."

Their gratitude embarrassed Joshua. He had learned to swim at the same time he had learned to crawl, or so his mother had said. He hadn't thought about saving anyone. He'd just done it. He shrugged. "Don't worry about it."

"The Chinaboy ought to worry," said Toby, scowling at Yutang. "He nearly drowned us."

Yutang looked at his feet. "I am sorry for that."

"And you could've stayed out of it," Toby told Joshua.

Joshua shrugged again. "I tried to. But I couldn't."

Toby opened his mouth as if to speak, then looked away.

Joshua told himself he didn't care what the white boy did. Once they got to the wharf, he would never see Toby or Yutang again. He called to the blond man, "I appreciate your pulling us out, sir."

"Always glad to be of service, lad," the blond man said. "I'm Augustus, by the way. I overheard you're Toby, and you're Joshua." He looked at Yutang. "Who're you?"

"Lin Yutang," Yutang answered, nodding shyly.

Joshua asked Augustus, "Where are you from?"

Augustus laughed. "Just about anyplace you can imagine. You ask Captain Malachi. He'll tell you what you'd like to know."

As the boat came up beside the strange ship, the red-coated men drew in their oars. A rope ladder with wooden rungs fell to meet them. Augustus caught the ladder, then turned to the boys. "Who's first?"

Toby said, "Me!" He scrambled upward,

using his clawlike right hand as easily as his left. Yutang hurried after him.

Joshua stroked Lincoln, who stood unsteadily looking up at him. Joshua wondered if he could carry the dog in one arm and climb with the other. He hated to think of falling into the sea again.

The blond man said, "We can hoist your dog up with the boat."

"Thanks." Joshua patted Lincoln and said, "Stay!" Lincoln whimpered a feeble protest, then lay down as if he would really rather be napping, anyway. Joshua scurried up the ladder.

Another little man in a suit waited by the ship's rail. His hair and beard were long and white, but he looked enough like Augustus to be his brother. He smiled at Joshua. "Welcome aboard the *Basset*! I'm Sebastian, the first mate."

"Thank you, sir." Joshua stepped onto the deck by the other two boys.

The ship seemed remarkably tidy, as if it were ready for an inspection by royalty. Joshua looked back to see Augustus and the red-coated rowers climbing the rope ladder. At the rail, several more tiny red-coated men pulled on a winch to raise the boat holding Lincoln. More of the tiny crewmen scrambled up the three masts, clearly getting ready to drop the sails.

Joshua tried to guess how many of the crewmen there were, but couldn't. They moved too quickly and looked too similar to keep them separate.

But he saw five of the larger men in dark suits, counting Augustus from the boat and Sebastian who had waited by the ladder. They all had whiskers. One, standing on the high rear deck by the ship's steering wheel, had a salt-and-pepper beard that reminded Joshua of pictures of President Grant. He was talking to a slightly taller little man with a red beard but no mustache. The last little man, on the forward deck directing the red-coated crew as they scurried about, had an enormous white mustache that hid his mouth and chin—a real soup-strainer, Joshua thought, wanting to laugh.

As he and the other boys gawked at the spectacle of a sailing ship preparing to depart, the red-bearded man strode down from the rear deck. He said in a deep, booming voice, "Welcome aboard! I'm Captain Malachi." He waved toward Sebastian. "And this is my first mate, Sebastian."

Sebastian bowed. "Pleased to meet you." He glanced at his captain and added, "All *three* of you."

Malachi nodded at the blond man with the goatee. "You already met Seaman Augustus."

Augustus grinned. "A rather soggy introduction."

Joshua grinned back. Half of his attention was
on the crewmen swinging the rowboat on board,
and the dog peering over its side.

Beside Joshua, Yutang said, "Excuse me—"

"A moment, lad," Malachi said. "There are
two more of us I'd like to point out." He lifted his
arm toward the ship's wheel and the man with
the salt-and-pepper beard. "Archimedes there is
our helmsman."

Augustus said, "We all do a bit more than our
titles suggest."

Yutang said, a little louder, "Please—"

"Shh!" whispered Toby. "Don't Chinese have
any manners?"

Instead of answering, Yutang looked back at
the wharf with a worried expression. Joshua
didn't follow Yutang's gaze, because Lincoln
chose that moment to jump from the rowboat,
which the little men were still lowering into its
berth. To Joshua's relief, the dog landed on the
ship's deck, skidded only a little, and trotted over
for a pat.

Sebastian glanced at Lincoln, then at Malachi,
muttering, "*And* a dog."

Joshua said quickly, "Don't worry. Lincoln's
house-trained."

Malachi nodded and pointed at the small man

on the forward deck whose mustache hid half his face. "That's Eli, the bosun."

"Anything you need, you tell him," said Augustus. "He'll find someone to take care of it. Usually me."

"Please!" Yutang pointed behind them. "Look!"

Joshua turned. The wharf was sliding away from the ship. So was the city of San Francisco. He looked up. At the bow, one sail billowed, pulling the *Basset* away from everything he knew.

"You're leaving?" Toby asked.

He whirled to stare at the small men. Malachi held up his hands. "Let me explain—" he began.

"I must return," Yutang said.

"I'm afraid none of you can . . . . "

Every second carried the ship farther away. Joshua snapped his fingers for Lincoln to follow, then ran to the rail nearest the shore. The wharf and the shore were close enough that he might be able to fight through the waves to safety. But could Lincoln?

Toby and Yutang ran up beside him. Yutang cupped his hands and shouted, "Help! We are being kidnapped!"

No one looked their way. Perhaps the wind carried away Yutang's voice. But it was as if he were in a dream, Joshua thought, in which this

ship and everyone on board could not be seen or
heard by people in the real world.

He heard Toby say, almost admiringly, "The
Little People, they're tricky."

Joshua looked back. Malachi, Sebastian, and
Augustus walked toward them. On the rear deck,
Archimedes drew on the wheel, turning the ship
toward the open sea. On the forward deck, Eli
shouted for the tiny crewmen to make more sail.

Joshua glared at Malachi. "You kidnapped
us."

Sebastian shook his head, his white beard
swaying like Spanish moss in a breeze. "We'd
never do that."

Toby said, "Have you a better word for it?"

Seaman Augustus scratched his goatee. "He
has a point." When Malachi and Sebastian
frowned at him, he added, "But what do I know?"

Malachi said, "We're not kidnapping you."

Yutang said, "Then take us back to the wharf,
please."

Sebastian and Augustus both looked at
Malachi. He shook his head, saying, "I'm sorry.
Too much is at stake. Before I explain, would you
tell me your names?"

Joshua looked at the retreating shore and
wished he had tried his luck in the sea. Toby's
and Yutang's faces showed the despair that he
felt. The little men might be half the boys' size,

but counting the red-coated crew, there were far too many of them for three boys to overpower. And if they did take control of the ship, what would they do with it? He doubted the other two knew any more about sailing than he did.

Joshua shrugged. "I'm Joshua Green."

"Toby McGee," said Toby with a grimace.

"I am Lin Yutang, sir," said Yutang with a fierce glare.

Malachi turned to the other bearded men. "Does that suggest anything?"

Sebastian and Augustus answered almost at once: "Can't say it does," and "Not for me, Cap'n."

Joshua frowned. "Suggest what?"

"Suggest which one of you is supposed to sail with us."

Joshua blinked twice. "You only want one of us?"

Malachi nodded. "To be more precise, we only *need* one of you."

Toby said, "Take one of them. My mother can't feed my brothers and sisters without my pay."

Yutang said, "My parents will worry if I do not come home soon."

Joshua stroked Lincoln's side, knowing he was the only one who didn't have anyone besides the dog to miss him. Whatever these little men had in mind, they didn't seem cruel. And being on the *Basset* might be better than being homeless in San Francisco. "I'll go. You can take the others back."

Malachi studied Joshua sadly. "Volunteering doesn't make you the one. All three of you arrived at the same time."

Yutang said, "You were going to kidnap the first person who fell into the sea?"

"Not kidnap," Sebastian said. "Take—"

"'Kidnap' is a fair word," Malachi agreed. "And I'm more sorry than I can say. The *Basset* hasn't been in a situation like this before, and I pray we're never in one again. But we couldn't risk leaving behind the one we need. And we couldn't lose time with explanations when so much depends on us. We only knew that the one we need would reach the *Basset* at noon in San Francisco. If you hadn't fallen in together—"

"You're sure it's one of us?" asked Toby.

Augustus said, "Of course. It's noon. This is San Francisco. You're on board. That's what we do."

"*What's* what you do?" asked Joshua. How could each explanation make less sense than the one before?

"We help people," Sebastian answered, almost as if he were embarrassed about it.

"By kidnapping them," Yutang said.

"No," Augustus said. "In all my voyages, we've never carried off an unwilling passenger."

"And when you hear our mission," Malachi said, "we hope you'll agree to come with us. We'll have you back before anyone misses you."

If that's true, Joshua thought, *they'll only have time to sail out of the bay and back. But that's a mighty big if.*

Toby said, "You'll take us back if we don't agree?"

Malachi looked away, then nodded.

Sebastian said, "Captain! The risk—"

Malachi shrugged. "If none of them will come, how could any of them be the one?

Joshua said, "Why should we believe you?"

The little men looked at each other as if hoping one of them could answer that. But support for them came from the last place that Joshua expected.

Toby said, "I hear the Little People don't lie."

Joshua frowned at him. The Little People? His grandmother had told him an Iroquois story about magical little people who helped others. But he didn't believe in magic. And even if he did, these little men didn't look like Iroquois.

"You'll find liars in many places," Malachi said. "But rarely aboard the *Basset.*"

Yutang said, "You said much is at risk?"

Malachi nodded.

Yutang said, "What will happen if none of us is the one you want?"

Sebastian said, "A war will break out. A terrible war, perhaps the most terrible war that has ever been fought."

Yutang nodded. "If you tell the truth—"

"We do," Malachi said.

"I agree to help," Yutang finished.

"Bless you, lad!" said Sebastian. Augustus grabbed Yutang's hand and pumped it, saying, "Good fellow!" Malachi nodded, saying, "Thank you."

The little men looked at Toby next. He asked, "Is there a reward?"

Augustus laughed. "You don't return on the *Basset* with treasure."

"Only memories," said Sebastian.

Toby shrugged. "Well. It's a free trip."

Malachi said, "It won't cost money, anyway."

"And you swear I'll be back before anyone knows I've gone?"

"We do."

"Then I'm willing to help."

Sebastian smiled and squeezed Toby's right hand. Toby looked a little embarrassed, but Sebastian didn't seem to notice anything unusual about the hand. Augustus said, "You won't regret it," and Malachi repeated his simple "Thank you."

Joshua thought it would be over then, but Malachi looked at him. "You said you would come. But that, I think, was to spare these boys. Are you still willing?"

"I haven't changed my mind," Joshua said. And as the three little men shook his hand and thanked him, he thought about being kidnapped by tiny men in an old-fashioned sailing ship to go somewhere to prevent a war. *I must be crazy,* he thought, *or dreaming.*

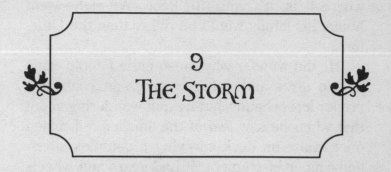

9
THE STORM

Toby liked the wind and the surge of the ship beneath his feet as it leaped across the waves, speeding away from San Francisco. He liked watching Joshua's dog delightedly sniffing the ship and the little men. He liked the way the crew paused to scratch Lincoln at the back of his head or behind his floppy ears. If Nick Finney or Elizabeth O'Leary or one of his brothers or sisters could be along, this trip would be perfect. The only thing he didn't like was having to put up with Joshua and the Chinaboy.

The officers of the *Basset* had said they would return before anyone missed them, so he wasn't worried about his family or his job. His mother had told him stories of Ireland and the Little People and their magic. They might try to trick you, but they never lie. They each have a pot of gold hidden at the end of a rainbow, and if you learn where it is, it's yours to keep. When he went home, his family would be richer than the Littletons.

He did wonder why these Little People came in two sizes and didn't wear green coats like proper leprechauns, but he quit wondering about that when he saw two of the smaller red-coated ones come on deck carrying a complex silver-and-copper instrument. It had gears and wheels and arrows and dials and a thousand parts, like a music box or a clockwork amusement from a carnival or a fun house. Seeing them take the device toward the rear deck, Toby called, "Captain Malachi! What's that?"

The captain grinned. "You'll see, m'lad."

Malachi led Toby, Joshua, and Yutang up onto the rear deck. Two red-coated crewmen were handling the wheel under the supervision of the helmsman with the salt-and-pepper beard. Malachi called, "Archimedes! Our passengers, Joshua, Yutang, and Toby!"

Archimedes shook their hands, saying, "Delighted. Enjoying your trip so far?"

Toby nodded. "Being kidnapped and standing around in wet clothes are two of my favorite things."

Archimedes stared at him, then laughed.

"Someone'll get you some dry clothes soon enough."

Malachi coughed into his hand, then said, "Thought they'd like to see the *wuntarlabe* first."

"That is a voon-ter-lob?" Yutang pointed at the strange machine, pronouncing the word much like the small man had.

"Indeed," Malachi said. Several red-coated men were gathering around the device. Malachi asked them, "Whose turn is it?"

One tiny man laughed and ran forward, pressing his nose against the side of the machine.

Malachi told the boys in professorial tones, "Use a dwarf to set the *wuntarlabe* and a gremlin to spin its wheels."

The words rang like cannon fire in Toby's ears. *Dwarf? Gremlin?* Not leprechauns? Joshua did not seem to share his confusion; he only grinned. Yutang frowned and asked, "What is a gremlin?"

"One of the crew," Archimedes said. "Didn't they tell you?"

Malachi, looking apologetic, said, "Seemed there were more important things to tell." He turned to the boys and gestured toward himself and Archimedes. "We're dwarves." He swept his arm toward the nearest red-coated crewmen. "They're gremlins."

Yutang, still frowning, said, "I knew *dwarf* was the English word for little people. I thought the others were midgets."

"No," said Malachi. "Midgets are human."

"Dwarves," Joshua said. "Like in fairy tales?"

Archimedes nodded.

Joshua laughed as if he had suddenly understood something. "Of course!"

"You are not human?" Yutang said carefully.

Malachi shook his head.

Toby asked hopefully, "Are gremlins and dwarves different kinds of leprechauns?"

"No, lad." Archimedes chuckled and added, "You hardly ever see a leprechaun at sea."

Yutang said, "We are to believe that?"

"Certainly," said Archimedes. "They hate the water."

"I *meant*," Yutang said more carefully, "you think we will believe that you are dwarves and gremlins? Not humans?"

"Of course," said Malachi. "It's crucial." He pointed at a banner flying from the tallest mast. "See that?"

Yutang read it aloud. "*Credendo vides*. What's that mean?"

Malachi said, "It's Latin for 'By believing, one sees.'"

"Sees what?" asked Toby. He wondered why Joshua thought this was all amusing. When Toby had thought he was among leprechauns, this was a grand adventure. Now nothing made sense, and that frightened him.

"In this case, by believing, you'll see our destination," said Malachi. "The land of the Norse gods."

"Norway?" said Toby. "That's thousands of miles away!"

"The Norse gods weren't known only in Scandinavia," said Archimedes. "Long ago, people told stories about them from Russia to Great Britain."

Yutang said, "So you say we are sailing to Europe. But we'll be back before anyone notices we're gone."

Joshua laughed and shook his head. "Why not?"

Archimedes said patiently, "Not Europe. The lands of myth. They're very near when you sail with the *Basset*."

"Myth?" Yutang asked.

"Things that don't exist," Joshua explained.

"Unless you believe," added Malachi. "The *wuntarlabe* guides us by belief."

Joshua grinned. "Dwarves, gremlins, myths, and a—a *wonder-lob*."

Yutang frowned at him, then said, "I think

maybe mad circus performers have stolen a ship."

Toby said, "He's not mad. This is magic."

Yutang said, "That's impossible."

"Sure," said Toby. "Like not noticing a ship right in front of your eyes. Or falling off a dock and having a boat come so fast it must've been waiting for you. Or sailing into the wind. This whole trip's impossible."

Joshua and Yutang glanced up at the billowing sails. Yutang's frown deepened. Toby said, "You didn't notice?"

Yutang turned his frown to Toby. "I never sailed before—"

Malachi sighed and turned to the tiny red-coated man standing by the *wuntarlabe*. "What's in your hat?"

The man grinned, pulled off his tall hat, and began emptying it. He pulled out three sandwiches, each made from a loaf of French bread, then a rolled-up drawing of a mechanical bird, then a red-and-yellow umbrella, then three books, then a pair of skis, then a large black ball with three holes in one side, then a music box—

"That's enough," said Malachi. "Thanks."

The gremlin laughed and began putting the things back in his hat.

"It's magic," Yutang said in wonder.

"It's impossible," Joshua stated with another laugh.

Toby couldn't take his eyes off the gremlin's hat. "What else have you got in there?"

Malachi said, "There isn't time for him to show you everything." He nodded to the gremlin, who giggled, put his finger in a depression in the *wuntarlabe*'s silver-and-copper wheel, and spun it.

The wheel became a blur. Dials whirled, bells tinkled, and the *wuntarlabe* shook so fiercely that Toby thought it would shake itself apart. Then, with a final *tock*ing of gears snapping into place and a bell *ping*ing to say that it was done, the central arrow of the *wuntarlabe* pointed straight ahead of the ship.

"That's it?" Toby expected something amazing, the skies cracking open or an island rising up out of the sea. But as far as he could tell, the ship sailed on like before, no faster, no slower, and not changing course the tiniest bit.

"Hardly," said Archimedes.

Yutang stared past the prow. "Where did the fog come from?"

Toby looked ahead, where Yutang stared. The blue sky ended in a gray curtain of fog. It rolled rapidly toward the *Basset*. Within seconds, it encased the ship so thickly that Toby could not see more than a few feet ahead of the prow. He shivered in his damp clothes as the sunlight disappeared.

Joshua said, "Shouldn't you wait out the fog?"

"Not when lives depend on us," said Malachi.

Before Toby could ask whether the dwarves cared about *their* lives, Archimedes nodded at the *wuntarlabe*. The needle continued to point toward the prow. "Fog doesn't matter. We're on course."

Joshua nodded. "I forgot. Who cares if you hit something in a dream?"

The *Basset* shuddered as though it had scraped a sandbar.

"What did you say?" Malachi asked. He used the same calm voice that Toby's mother had once used when he said a swear word, so he knew something was very wrong.

Joshua said, "I just meant it can't hurt to run into something when you're dreaming."

Overhead, the sails snapped as if the wind had changed direction. The masts groaned.

"You're not dreaming," Malachi said, even more calmly.

Joshua laughed. "Dwarves and gremlins and a ship sailing into the wind? I've got to be either crazy or dreaming."

The *Basset* lurched as if a wave had hit it from the starboard side. Toby grabbed a rail to keep his balance. One gremlin fell away from the wheel and skidded across the deck. The wheel spun, carrying the second gremlin around it. Archimedes caught the wheel and held it steady. His face was as white as the sails overhead.

A gremlin ran to Archimedes and shouted something over the growing roar of the winds buffeting the ship. Toby noticed that the gremlin wasn't smiling. He glanced around. None of the gremlins were smiling.

Archimedes shouted to Malachi, "We're taking on water!"

The ship's creaks and groans grew louder. Caught between the waves and the winds, it rolled from side to side. Toby and Yutang grabbed onto ropes. Lincoln whimpered at Joshua, who shifted his weight from one leg to the other to stay upright. He looked up into the rigging and the gray sky beyond and said, "I always imagined storms were like this!"

Archimedes shouted, "I'm sure you did! Imagine something different!"

"Why?" said Joshua. "I'll wake up soon if this gets too scary."

Malachi said, "This is real!"

"But this is impossible!" Joshua shouted back.

"Here, the impossible is normal!" Malachi answered. "That's how you get to the lands of wonder! By believing what's impossible!"

"That doesn't make sense!" Joshua said.

Toby looked up. High overhead, a sail ripped free and flapped in the wind. Gremlins hung on to the crosstrees like desperate monkeys. One lost his grip with his legs and swung from side to side in the wind like a living flag. Toby shouted, "It's not a dream, you fool!"

"Well," Joshua said, "I never had a white boy call me a fool in a dream before—"

"It ought to happen more often!" Toby said.

Joshua glared at Toby. "This dream may get better if the ship sinks."

"If we all drown?" asked Yutang. "Even you? Even Lincoln?"

Joshua's anger disappeared and he glanced at Lincoln.

Toby said, "I hear you die in your sleep if you die in a dream."

"I doubt that," said Joshua, sounding less sure of himself.

A wave rolled across the deck, drenching them all. "Will you stop doubting things!" Malachi bellowed.

Toby caught Lincoln to keep him from washing overboard. Frightened, Lincoln struggled in his arms. Archimedes, Malachi, and a gremlin clung to the ship's wheel, fighting to hold it steady. The central arrow of the *wuntarlabe* spun in wild circles, somehow pointing in every direction except the one that the ship was heading.

A second wave swept across the deck. As it crashed over him, Toby lost sight of everyone. Lincoln was only a struggling furry mass against his side. When the wave rolled away, Toby saw that Joshua had fallen and caught the rail near the stairs to the lower deck.

Malachi shouted, "We can't go back, Joshua! You must believe!"

"I'm going to wake up," Joshua insisted. "Now!"

If they were trapped in a dream, Toby thought, it was a nightmare. He shouted, "You're going to wreck us!"

Joshua stared at him, then looked out at the storm.

"Do you want us to die?" Yutang asked, keeping an arm through the railing. "Even in a dream?"

"Of course not!"

"Look at Lincoln. He's terrified."

"But what can I do?"

"Believe!"

"You can't just believe!"

"Are you so sure this is a dream that you would let us drown?"

"No!"

"Then you already believe a little."

"But I don't think—"

Yutang clapped a hand over Joshua's mouth. "In your dream, believe this is real."

Joshua stared at him, then nodded. Yutang brought down his hand.

"I'm on a ship," Joshua said while the wood of the *Basset* screamed as if the ship would tear itself apart in the storm. "The ship is crewed by dwarves and gremlins. We're sailing through something impossible to—"

"Somewhere impossible," Malachi suggested.

"Somewhere impossible," Joshua agreed. "That's what's happening."

The winds grew calmer. Above them, the gremlin who had been flapping like a flag managed to wrap his legs around the mast.

"You believe that, here and now?" said Yutang.

"I believe that, here and now," Joshua agreed.

And the sea became as flat as glass, and the *wuntarlabe* pointed straight into the mist.

"It's that easy?" Toby asked in amazement. The storm had faded as quickly as any dream. He wondered for an instant if Joshua had been right all along. Then he looked at the *Basset*. The decks were slick with water. Sails and ropes had torn free and flapped in the wind. One gremlin, with a very annoyed expression, held his hat upside down over the rail. Gallons of water poured out of it.

"If you call this easy," Malachi answered. He looked across the sodden deck and shouted, "Eli, take our passengers to their cabins!" He nodded at the boys. "You'll find dry clothes there." With that, Malachi left and began calling compliments and orders to the crew, who were already replacing sails and ropes.

Toby let go of Lincoln, who ran like a puppy to Joshua to lick his face. Joshua laughed and told the dog, "Boy, your breath's too bad for this to be a dream," and let him lick him some more.

Joshua turned, staring at the damage from the storm. "All this because I said—" he began.

Without thinking, Toby clapped a hand over Joshua's mouth at the same time Yutang did.

"Yes," said Yutang. "What you say affects what you think."

Toby looked at Yutang and thought that maybe not all Chinese were alike. He said, "You're pretty smart, for a Chinaboy."

"Smarter than you," said Joshua. "Did you really think it'd help to call me a fool?"

Yutang gave Toby a small smile. "Under the circumstances, perhaps not the wisest thing—"

"As if you'd know," Toby snapped, hurt that someone he had just called smart would call him stupid.

Joshua shrugged. "I know a fool when *I* hear one."

I should've known they'd team up, Toby thought. "Oh, yeah?" he said. "Everyone sounds foolish to a fool."

"You'd know," Joshua said.

"You're the one who nearly drowned us—" Toby began.

"Please!" Yutang said. "Why do barbarians always bicker?"

Toby turned to Yutang, but Joshua spoke first. "Barbarians?"

Yutang covered his mouth with his hand. "I'm sorry. It is not your fault that you are not Chinese. It—"

"Why would I want to be, Chinaboy?" Joshua said coldly.

Watching the two boys glare at each other, Toby laughed. Joshua whirled toward him. "What's so funny, lobster-hand?"

Toby jerked his maimed hand into his damp pocket. He had forgotten about being crippled for as long as he had been on the *Basset,* for longer than he had ever forgotten about it. As he replied, he heard the shrill pitch of his voice, but he didn't care what he sounded like. "Even with one hand, I'm better than either of you—"

Eli, at the hatch, said, "You all done with your spat?"

Toby decided not to answer until one of the others did. They must have decided the same thing.

Eli said, "The *Basset*'s a peaceful ship. You want to stay on board, you abide by the rules. You're always welcome to swim home if you want. Maybe that's how we'll know who's the one we want. Well? Anyone want to be fish bait?"

Toby might not like Joshua or Yutang, but he didn't need to fight them. He only had to put up with them until the trip was over. "I won't start anything."

"Me neither," Joshua agreed. But his voice wasn't friendly, and Lincoln, by his side, watched Toby and Yutang warily.

Yutang inhaled deeply, then said, "I follow the way of peace."

Joshua said, "That's why your fists are balled up?"

Yutang looked at his hands, then unclenched them and turned to Eli. "Show me my quarters. It is easier to be peaceful when I am not surrounded by"—his hesitation was very brief, but very clear—"others."

Yutang started down the stairs from the stern deck. Toby followed, feeling colder and more miserable than when he had been fished out of the ocean with the other boys. At least he knew who to blame: Yutang, for knocking them into

the water in the first place, and Joshua, for causing the storm.

Eli threw the main hatch wide to reveal stairs
into the ship, lit by the flickering light of gas
lanterns. "This way," he grunted, then headed
down, muttering, "My, this'll be a fun voyage."

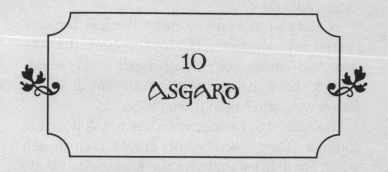

10
ASGARD

Yutang thought about Toby and Joshua as he followed Eli down a long corridor of gleaming wood lit by gas lamps. The Pirate King would have told the barbarians to stop their tongues, or he would stop them forever. But the Pirate King would not be on the *Basset* in the first place. The Pirate King didn't care about anyone, and certainly not barbarians—he never would have gone back to help Joshua on the wharf.

As he walked, Yutang listened to Eli identifying the doors they passed: "That's the library, but you won't have time to read. That's the galley, but you won't have time to eat. That's the gymnasium, but you'll be getting enough exercise when we arrive. Here you go. Dress quickly, because we're nearly there." Before Yutang could ask a

question, Eli left the boys standing in front of
three cabin doors.

Yutang looked farther down the hall. It disappeared into shadows. He looked back the way
they had come. Something didn't make sense.
With a shock, he realized that the inside of the
Basset was larger than the outside.

He turned to Joshua and Toby to ask how that
could be. They looked coldly at him, then at each
other. He didn't want to be the first one to speak.
Neither, apparently, did they. Besides, the answer
to his question was simple: It was magic.

He turned away from Joshua and Toby and
entered the nearest cabin. It was as large as his
family's carpentry shop. The cabin was bright, all
shining wood with polished brass fixtures. Dry
woolen clothes—black trousers, a red shirt, a
blue jacket—and leather boots like moccasins
waited on the bed. They looked strange, but
warm, and warm seemed more important than
strange just then.

Dressing quickly, he found that the clothes fit
perfectly, which led to a disturbing thought:
Would the same clothes have waited for him if he
had gone into another cabin? Or had the dwarves
known which cabin he would pick? Or had they
somehow made sure that he picked this one? He
shook his head to chase away the questions.

Wondering about magic only made his head hurt.

When he came back on deck, the fog had disappeared. Directly overhead, the sun shone brightly down on the ship. The air was cold and crisp and, under the tang of the sea, smelled faintly of pine trees. Directly ahead of the *Basset* lay a green island with rocky cliffs and snow-capped mountains.

"Asgard," Malachi said, as if that was explanation enough.

Joshua called from the prow, "A ship!" He, too, wore strange new clothes: black moccasins, brown trousers, a yellow shirt, and a red jacket.

Yutang looked where Joshua pointed. A low, dark shape like a sea serpent raced from the island.

"That's Freyr's ship, *Skidbladnir*," Malachi announced with a nod. "Freyr will take you the rest of the way."

"Not you?" Toby walked up from the stern, dressed like the other boys, though his moccasins were gray, his trousers blue, his shirt green, and his jacket black.

"*Skidbladnir* can carry you faster than we could."

"So why didn't it fetch us in the first place?" Toby asked.

"Because it doesn't belong in your world."

"Our world?" asked Yutang. "We are in another world?"

"Here, they think there are nine worlds counting Earth, which they call Midgard." Malachi pointed into the distance, where the clouds had cleared away, and an arc of many colors crossed the sky. "See that rainbow? It's the Bifrost Bridge. They could've walked over it to find you, but that would've taken longer than sending the *Basset*." Malachi laughed. "And they might've gotten lost. No one from here has visited Midgard in centuries."

As the sea serpent came near, Yutang saw that it was a low, slender ship with a single mast, a billowing sail, and two banks of long oars speeding back and forth. Round shields lined its sides. A painted wooden dragon's head adorned its prow.

It pulled up beside the *Basset,* matching its speed. One person walked *Skidbladnir*'s deck: a tall, handsome blond man whose cloak, tunic, trousers, and boots were all shades of green. He shouted with a deep, carrying voice like an actor's, "Good day, Captain Malachi! You made good time!"

"The best we could, Freyr!" Malachi shouted back. "I hope it's good enough!"

"Send over our champion," Freyr answered,

"and we'll find out!"

"You'll have to take three!" Malachi swept his hand toward Yutang, Joshua, and Toby.

Freyr frowned. "Boys?"

Malachi smiled.

Freyr's frown deepened. "No warriors?"

Malachi shook his head.

Freyr's frown grew even deeper. "You're sure of this?"

Malachi nodded again. "They came to the *Basset* at noon in San Francisco."

As Freyr studied the boys, a terrible thought occurred to Yutang: What if the one they needed had been walking along the wharf, about to reach the *Basset* just when the boys had fallen into the sea? If Malachi had made the wrong decision by carrying them away, people would die. And the fault would ultimately be Yutang's, because his tackling Toby and Joshua had made them all fall in.

"Boys," Freyr repeated.

If Malachi suspected something had gone wrong, his voice stayed confident. He asked, "Have we made a mistake before?"

"Never, but—" Freyr shook his head as if shaking away his doubts. "Either Asgard will be saved or we shall all die gloriously." He looked back at the boys. "Which is the lord and which are his serfs?"

"No lord and no serfs!" Malachi said.

"Our hero brought his friends? Or his brothers?"

Yutang wondered how well Freyr could see, if he thought such different-looking boys could be brothers. As for friends, well, it was too late to think either Toby or Joshua could ever be his friend.

"We don't know which one's yours! That's why you get them all!"

Freyr stared. "Malachi—"

"They met the requirements. One of them must be your hero."

Freyr shrugged. "Better too many than too few, I suppose! Come aboard, lads!"

As several gremlins ran out a plank from the *Basset* to *Skidbladnir,* Malachi looked at the boys. "Don't worry. We'll be waiting to take you home."

Yutang realized he was reluctant to leave the *Basset.* The dwarves had treated them well. He wondered how Freyr would treat them. Then Freyr stooped and clapped his hands. Joshua's gray dog ran across the plank to lick the blond man's fingers. That, Yutang decided, had to be a good sign.

"Lincoln!" Joshua cried, running after the dog. Toby shrugged and followed Joshua, sauntering as if he did this every day. Yutang nodded to Malachi and walked casually toward the gang-plank. He stepped onto it and felt it shift beneath his feet. Glancing down, he saw waves splash together in the narrow space between the ships. He did not like heights, and he could not swim. He tried not to think about what would happen if a gust of wind blew the ships apart while he was on the plank—or what would happen if a gust blew the ships together and he fell between their hulls.

The wind stayed steady. Yutang stepped down onto *Skidbladnir*'s deck with a sigh of relief, and the gremlins pulled back the plank. All five dwarves gathered along the *Basset*'s rail to shout "Good luck!" which Yutang knew they were supposed to hear, followed by Eli's mut-tered "They'll need it," which he suspected they were not. As the dwarves waved their hands and the gremlins waved their hats, Yutang realized that he would miss them.

Toby and Joshua had begun looking around Freyr's long ship, and Lincoln was sniffing his way from one end to the other. Yutang saw many benches, but no rowers.

Toby said, "It's like a painting I saw of a Viking ship. Only where's the crew?"

Freyr grinned at him and called, "To Asgard!" The oars began rowing by themselves, speeding

Skidbladnir away from the *Basset*. The long ship skimmed the top of the waves like a sea bird swooping low in search of fish.

More magic, Yutang thought. Did people in Asgard take magic for granted? Or did they see something like Freyr's ship in the same way that Yutang saw a train or a steamship in his world, as a beautiful and awesome thing created from someone's imagination?

Freyr smiled at him, which made Yutang realize that his mouth hung open as he gawked at the oars. Freyr said, "Dwarves made *Skidbladnir*. It needs no rowers. It goes where I want."

"Why's the *Basset* have a crew, then?" asked Joshua. "Didn't dwarves make it, too?"

"The *Basset* is what it is," said Freyr. "Its dwarves are smaller and friendlier than those in Nidavellir. Their magic must be different, too."

Yutang looked back. The *Basset* dwindled behind *Skidbladnir*. This ship's deck did not roll beneath his feet. It vibrated as it shot across the waves so quickly that he was not sure whether it sailed or flew.

The island's rocky cliffs grew larger before him. He admired its enormous green forests, a wide river flowing into the sea, and steep mountains with snowy peaks. Far in the distance, he thought he saw a tree so tall that it reached into the heavens. That, he decided, had to be a trick of the mountains and the clouds.

"Asgard," Freyr announced with pride and sorrow in his voice. "My adopted home."

"Adopted?" asked Joshua.

"I was born one of the Vanir. I lived in Vanaheim until I joined the Aesir of Asgard. Vanaheim is a gentler place than Asgard."

"What brought you here?" asked Yutang. "Do you have to work to support your family in Vanaheim?"

Freyr shook his head sadly. "Asgard is my home. The Vanir and the Aesir went to war long ago, because—well, it seemed important then. But now we live together in peace." He pointed toward a golden ribbon of beach along the wild shore. "There's a true son of Asgard. Perhaps the truest of all."

A huge, muscular man with long red hair and a thick red beard waited on the beach in a chariot harnessed to two large, hairy animals, one black and one white. Before Yutang could look more closely, he noticed that *Skidbladnir* still surged toward the shore without slowing. If the ship's speed changed at all, in fact, it flew faster. He swallowed, then tried not to sound like he was afraid. "Excuse me, Mr. Freyr, but if we do not slow down—"

Toby glanced at the beach and shouted, "Brace yourselves!" He dropped to the deck and grabbed a rower's bench. Joshua, near him, seized another bench and shouted, "Lincoln! Here!"

"I've got him!" Yutang threw one arm around Lincoln's neck and knelt to clutch a bench like the others. He pressed the gray dog close to him, ready to protect it with his body. As Lincoln's chest rose and fell against his, Yutang stared ahead. He felt the wind whip his queue behind him, like the flying braids in Freyr's hair.

Freyr stayed standing in the center of the ship with his feet far apart and his fists on his hips. "Be at ease! What use is a ship that destroys itself at the end of every voyage?"

Skidbladnir seemed to be slowing down. Yutang looked over the side, expecting to see water. The ship glided over the sands, touching the earth as lightly as it had touched the sea.

"And *Skidbladnir* is a most useful ship," Freyr added smugly.

The ship slid to a gentle stop. Without warning, it began shrinking, lowering its passengers onto the sand as it silently folded in on itself. In a moment, they all stood on the ground.

Yutang gasped. How did anyone ever get used to magic? Lincoln took several steps back across the beach, then whirled, ran thirty feet away, and began barking at the folded ship that lay at Freyr's feet like a playing card. Toby laughed, but Yutang recognized the nervous laugh that hides shock or fear. Joshua glanced from side to side with wide eyes, and Yutang realized that he must have had the same expression.

Freyr picked up the folded ship and tucked it into a pocket, declaring, "Useful indeed."

The man in the chariot said, "Move aside, boys. I wish to see who has come to save us!"

Freyr said, "You see them."

The stranger frowned. He was taller and more muscular than anyone Yutang had ever seen. In any other place, he would have thought the man must be a carnival strongman. His hair and his beard were golden red, like the sun at sunset. He wore an orange tunic, a fur cape the color of clouds, and high black fur boots. The shaggy beasts harnessed to the chariot were enormous, angry-looking mountain goats—one white, one black, both with fierce curved horns.

"I only see those boys."

"That's right."

Redbeard's puzzlement grew deeper, then disappeared as his eyes opened wide in shock or horror or disbelief. "Not—"

Freyr nodded. "Malachi assures me it's so."

Redbeard furled his brow. "These three puny lads?"

Freyr nodded.

Redbeard glowered at them. Yutang found

himself inching closer to Toby and noticed Joshua stepping closer to him.

Suddenly the man's face cracked into a smile. Then he laughed. His entire body shook, and so, it almost seemed, did the earth around him. "That's funny, Freyr! I'd expect a joke from Loki, but not from you!" He looked around the beach. "So where's the hero hiding? It's a bad time to jest. Odin has called a council to discuss war."

"It's no jest. These are the *Basset*'s passengers."

Redbeard scratched his chin, then pointed at the boys. "You're pretending to be boys!"

Freyr shook his head. "I'm sure they're just boys. The *Basset* brought them from Midgard."

"Hmm." Redbeard scratched his chin some more. "We could cut off their heads and see if they turn into something else!"

Yutang looked at Joshua and Toby and saw them look at him. Like him, they were trying not to look scared. They weren't succeeding, which made him suspect that he wasn't, either.

Freyr said, "Do you want to tell Odin that you killed our champion because you thought he might turn into something else?"

"No," Redbeard said. "If you think they're only boys, they're probably only boys. You're a smart one, Freyr."

As Freyr nodded with a slight smile, Redbeard addressed the boys. "Which of you came to help us?"

"I did," Toby said.

"So did I," said Joshua.

"I, too," said Yutang, pleased that his voice came out as strong as Toby's and Joshua's.

"Huh." Redbeard resumed his chin-scratching. "Which of you do we want?"

"Me," said Toby. Then he glanced at the others and said, "Well, probably me."

"I caused us to fall into the sea," Yutang said reluctantly. "I am likely the one you seek."

"I was the first to agree to this," Joshua protested. "I bet it's me."

"Three human boys," Redbeard said glumly. "And we don't even know which one."

"Is that our problem?" Freyr asked. "The *Basset* sends three; we take three. Let Odin and Loki and Freyja ponder it."

Redbeard grinned. "Three means we can lose two and still have one left!"

Yutang gulped and Joshua blinked. Toby scowled and said, "No one's losing me."

"No, lad," Freyr said. "We've lost enough already."

Yutang said, "We are here to find something that was lost?"

Freyr nodded. "Freyja promised that in her prophesy."

He wanted to ask if Freyr really believed in prophesies. But the longer this trip lasted, the harder it was to assume that anything might be impossible. Yutang simply asked, "Freyja?"

"My sister," Freyr answered.

Joshua said, "What's gone missing? Maybe we can find it right off, and Mr. Freyr can get us back to the *Basset.*"

Redbeard frowned more deeply than before, more deeply than Yutang had seen any person frown. A shadow fell across the beach. Yutang looked up. A black storm cloud filled the sky, which had been clear only a moment before. Yutang glanced at Joshua and saw Toby glance at him, too.

Joshua frowned at them and shook his head as if to say, "I'm not doing that!"

"Someone stole my hammer!" Redbeard growled, and lightning flashed across the sky.

Freyr put a hand on Redbeard's shoulder. "We'll find it."

"If Freyja was right."

"Has she ever been wrong?" Freyr asked as if the idea was an insult, making Yutang wonder if the Vanir and the Aesir were as friendly as Freyr had suggested.

Joshua cleared his throat. "Where was the last place you used your hammer?"

The two men stared at him. Then Redbeard

laughed. "Two giants came near Asgard's walls. I threw the hammer to scare them back."

"Then it is probably lying where you threw it," Yutang suggested.

Redbeard shook his head. "When I throw Mjollnir, it always returns to my hand."

"You're Thor!" said Joshua.

"Of course!" He frowned at Freyr. "A boy that ignorant can't be the one."

Freyr shrugged. "None of them knows us. Midgard has changed since we visited it."

"They don't know me?" asked Thor. "Do they know anything?"

"Thor," said Joshua. "Norse god of thunder. Thursday's named for you." When Yutang looked at him, Joshua explained, "I read about the days of the week in a *Farmer's Almanac*."

"Ah!" Thor grinned at Freyr. "I still have a day."

Freyr shrugged. "Freyja has Friday, Odin Wednesday, Tyr Tuesday. We're not forgotten."

"What do days matter?" Thor spoke as if he didn't care, but Yutang heard his happiness. He reached for his reins. "Deeds matter! Come! To Odin's hall!"

Freyr leaped into the chariot and beckoned to the boys. "Come on."

Yutang glanced at Joshua and Toby, then at the chariot. "There is not much room...."

"There's enough." Thor lifted the reins. "Time waits for no one, not even Thor!"

Yutang stepped up into the chariot. It creaked under his weight, a comforting sound in this place of magic. He liked the idea of traveling on solid ground for a change. As Toby, Joshua, and Lincoln scrambled up, Thor turned to the goats and called, "Ho, Tanngnost! Ho, Tanngrisni! To Valaskjalf, where Odin waits!"

The two fierce goats leaned into their harness. The chariot lurched forward. Its wooden wheels churned in the sand, digging deeper.

Yutang said, "Can they pull all of us in—"

The goats jumped, jerking the chariot off the ground. Yutang braced himself for the impact. But the goats kept pulling, drawing them higher and higher as if they raced along an invisible road into the sky. The green and rocky land fell away beneath them.

The Pirate King would command these barbarians to warn him whenever something magical was going to happen. Eyes closed, Yutang gripped the side of the chariot more tightly. He swallowed several times, hoping his stomach would stay down in his belly, rather than leap out of his throat as it seemed to want to do.

After a long moment, he dared to peek, and was glad to see that Toby's pale face seemed paler than before. But Joshua grinned into the wind, and Lincoln rested his front paws on the chariot's side as his ears blew back from his head.

"Buck up, lad!" Thor slapped Yutang's back. "If you fall, we'll catch you." Then he added, "Most likely!" and laughed as if he could imagine nothing funnier.

Yutang clapped his hand over his mouth. When he was sure that his stomach would stay in place, he asked, "Why did you not meet us on the *Basset?*"

Thor shrugged. "It's hard to land on the deck of a ship."

"And dwarves are finicky," Freyr added.

"Finicky?" Joshua asked.

The white goat dropped several round, dark turds. The wind whipped them beneath the chariot.

"Ah," said Yutang. "Finicky."

Watching the mountains and forests pass beneath them, he thought, *Such a hard land. Not like San Francisco*. They came to a wide plain where long-haired sheep grazed, and then flew over a high stone wall, taller than the trees growing near it.

Beyond the wall were a scattering of stone houses on a cliff overlooking a bay. The buildings looked like the homes of successful farmers, not gods. "Asgard?" Yutang asked.

Freyr nodded, then pointed at a gray spot in the green landscape. "And there's Valaskjalf!"

Yutang expected more from such a grand name. He had seen drawings in the newspaper of Chinese palaces and European castles. Valaskjalf looked like a hut built from rough stones and logs. As the chariot came closer, his opinion changed. Valaskjalf looked like a hut as big as a large church.

The goats landed in a clearing near Valaskjalf's front doors. The chariot bounced three times on its wooden wheels, jarring Yutang each time it struck the ground. Thor, Freyr, and Joshua grinned happily. Toby closed his eyes again, and Yutang kept his face still to hide how scared he was and how glad he was to be back on solid ground.

Yutang and Toby sprang out first. Toby caught Yutang's eye and smiled sheepishly. "Whew!" he whispered. Yutang closed his eyes and nodded in sympathy.

The others climbed down from the chariot. Lincoln sniffed the air and looked at Joshua, who said, "It's okay." The old dog wagged his tail, then greeted this new place by peeing on a tree.

Thor walked up to the oak doors, twice as tall as he was. "Come," he said impatiently. He wrenched the doors open wide, revealing a long hall as cool and as dark as a cave. "I'm back!" he called out. "With two more than we need!"

Someone in the shadowed room said in a pleasant voice, "Someday he'll return with exactly what was wanted. Our surprise will be so great that the world will end."

"Quiet, Loki," someone else said. The second voice came like a whisper from the far end of the building. Its tone, low and glum, made Yutang shiver.

Some light came from a huge fire in a huge fireplace. More came from torches along the wall. The smoky air made Yutang's eyes water. When they adjusted to the dimness, he saw that tall, tanned men and women stood at the far end of the hall. Perhaps half of them were armed. Firelight glinted on their swords and spears and helmets.

Their weapons made Yutang wonder if the Aesir had already voted for war. Most of the faces revealed no emotion as the newcomers approached. Doubt and confusion flickered across a few faces and was quickly replaced with distrust or disappointment.

A grim man with gray hair and a gray beard, who had a gray patch over one eye, sat in a massive stone chair at the end of the hall. A raven perched on each of his shoulders. A wolf lay on either side of his chair. The gray of his clothes was broken only by his blue cloak. Somehow, he seemed immensely tired and immensely strong at the same time.

Thor's laughter made the hall seem brighter. Many of the Aesir grinned at him. Most of them looked like him and Freyr—tall, pale, strong, with long, braided hair that ranged in color from snow blond to fire red.

The two exceptions were a dark-haired man dressed mostly in black and a slender blond man in red and black who was even taller than Thor. The tall man's face was handsome but harsh, with sharp cheekbones and a jutting jaw that could have been carved from the mountains by the wind.

Freyr nodded toward the one-eyed man in the stone chair. "That's Odin," he said quietly. "Our leader." He jerked his chin toward the tall man with the sharp face. "And Odin's brother, Loki."

"How've you been, Allfather?" Thor asked.

"Impatient," Odin answered. "And worried, too."

"Then stop worrying." Thor pointed at the boys. "Pick one you like. I'll throw the others back."

"We wanted a champion," Loki said with mild amusement. "And you brought us boys?"

A beautiful woman with hair as pale as Freyr's stepped forward. She wore a leather vest embossed with golden discs and carried two long spears. The top of her dress was the blue of the sea and the sky, the middle was the green of growing things, and the bottom was the brown of the earth. When she spoke, her voice was like music or running water. "The one we want is here. I feel his presence."

"My sister, Freyja," Freyr whispered for the boys.

Odin turned his one eye from Freyja to each boy. When Yutang was the subject of the gray man's gaze, he felt as if he were standing on an icy plain in the dead of winter.

The moment passed when Lincoln growled at the wolves. The wolves growled back, and Joshua caught Lincoln's scruff, saying, "Don't scare Mr. Odin's dogs!" Lincoln lay down, his ears suddenly flat. Yutang couldn't tell whether that was because of Joshua's command or the wolves' warning.

Odin said quietly, "Freki. Geri. They come to help us." The wolves stopped growling, but kept their yellow eyes on the boys. Yutang thought he would rather be up in Thor's chariot than in Valaskjalf.

Odin said, "Welcome to my hall. Tell me, what are your names and deeds?"

Toby swallowed nervously. "I'm Toby McGee, Mr. Odin. I haven't much in the way of deeds."

"What happened to your hand?" asked Loki.

Toby brushed his right hand against his leg. "A cutting machine."

"None of us has fought a machine that cuts," said Odin, with a tiny bit of hope or respect buried in his tone. He looked at Joshua next.

"I'm Joshua Green," Joshua declared. "I'm afraid I haven't done much, either." He saw Lincoln sniffing the feet of the frowning man dressed in black, and crooked a finger. Lincoln trotted back to him.

"Is that your dog?" Freyja asked.

"Well, Lincoln and I travel together." Joshua added hopefully, "I'm good with most creatures."

"Perhaps he'll tame the great wolf, Fenrir!" Loki said with a cool, mocking smile.

Loki's smile disappeared when Odin said, "Perhaps he will," and looked at Yutang.

"I am Lin Yutang." Yutang dipped his head in what he hoped would seem like a bow if a bow was expected, and a nod if one wasn't. "I have done no great deeds. But I will do what I can, if you need my help."

Loki said, "There's a claim anyone might make."

"But few do," Odin said. "A good answer, Lin Yutang."

Yutang blushed as Odin studied him. The

gray eye turned to Joshua, then Toby. Odin's ravens looked long and hard at the boys, too, and so did the wolves, and so did the assembled Aesir. No one seemed entirely pleased.

"Well?" said Thor. "Which should we keep, Allfather?"

Odin turned to Freyr's beautiful sister. "Freyja. You feel the promised one's presence?"

She looked at the boys. "He's here. I felt him just a short time ago, when he first set foot on Asgard. But I cannot tell which he is."

"Perhaps any of them will do," said Loki. "The longer we take to decide, the stronger our enemies become."

"Freyja spoke of only one," Odin said. "If we choose wrong now, we will have already lost."

Toby spoke up. "Anyone can see—" Every eye in the hall turned toward him, and he closed his mouth.

"Go on," Odin said.

Toby jerked his head at Yutang and Joshua. "You don't want them."

"Why not?"

"You're myths from Europe, right?"

"Myths?" Thor frowned. Yutang glanced up to see if the air would darken in Odin's hall, but apparently that only happened when Thor was *very* angry.

Toby said, "Gods. People worshiped you in Europe."

Loki smirked, and Odin's frown lightened so much that Yutang thought it must be the gray man's version of a smile. Thor nodded happily, saying, "Ah. True!"

"Well, Yutang's from China. Joshua's from Africa. They don't belong here."

Joshua said, "I'm from Alabama. Last I heard, that was in America."

"And I was born in San Francisco," Yutang said.

Toby said, "Sure, I was born in America, too. But my people came from Europe."

Joshua said, "I never heard the Irish worshiped Norse gods."

Toby pointed at the Aesir. "They were worshiped by white people." He tapped his chest and looked at Odin. "I'm the one you need."

Freyja said, "Why should the one we need look anything like us?"

Toby blinked at her, and Yutang was glad to see him blush. Toby stammered, "I just thought—"

"We need someone to help us, not worship us," Freyja said. "No one has worshiped us in nine centuries."

"I miss it," said Thor wistfully.

Freyr stepped forward. "My sister's prophesies have always come true. But we must consider the possibility that this time that will not be so. She spoke of one, not three."

Yutang felt a pang of guilt. He wanted to tell these people that he was sorry he knocked Toby and Joshua off the wharf, but he knew it was too late for apologies. Especially when the only effect would be to make everyone give up hope.

Freyr said, "The council should decide. Do we go to war?"

The dark-haired man in black spoke for the first time. "War with whom?" His voice was a low rumble. His right arm ended in a stump that was bound in black leather.

"That's Tyr," Freyr whispered to the boys. "War is his domain, just as storms are Thor's."

Thor said, "War with whom? The giants of Jotunheim, of course!"

"Did the giants take the hammer?" Tyr asked.

"Of course!" said Thor.

"Who saw that?" asked Tyr.

"No one!" said Thor. "They're sneaky!"

"Are they the only ones who are sneaky?"

"There's a foolish question!" Thor grinned. "Elves are sneaky, dwarves are sneaky—" His grin disappeared. "Oh."

Tyr asked, "Who gains the most if Asgard and Jotunheim go to war?"

"Didn't you hear me? The giants! Skrymir has

said he wants Asgard!"

Tyr said, as quietly as before, "People will die on both sides. One side will be destroyed, or greatly weakened. And with one or both of us destroyed or weakened, who gains, then?"

Thor opened his mouth to answer, closed it, opened it again, then kept it closed.

Loki, looking at Tyr with respect, said, "Perhaps the dwarves. Perhaps the elves."

Thor shook his head like a dog shaking off water and pointed at Loki. "You confuse everything, Trickster! This is simple. Giants tried to take my hammer before! This is their work!"

No one spoke for a moment. Freyr said, "Is it time to vote?"

"Is that necessary?" said Odin. "Except for Thor and Freyr, you wear your intentions."

Yutang looked at the men and women who had been in the hall when they arrived. He counted the ones with swords or spears: eleven. He counted those with no weapons: eleven, also. Tyr, god of war, with no sword on his hip or spear in his hand, was part of that group. So was Loki. Odin had no weapon on him, but a sword hung near his chair, so Yutang decided to wait to count him.

Thor said, "Skrymir of Jotunheim has wanted war long enough. I say give him his desire, and see how happy he is with it."

Odin nodded. Yutang thought, Twelve and eleven. With everyone else, he turned to Freyr.

Freyr nodded. "War."

Thirteen and eleven. War had won. Yutang looked at the Aesir. He did not know any of them, but he did not like to think of any of them dying.

Freyja threw her spears onto the floor. "If my prophesy was true, we were sent a boy, not a warrior, to be our hero. Perhaps we do not have to fight."

Odin said, "You vote for peace?"

Freyja nodded.

Twelve and twelve, Yutang thought. He saw everyone watching Odin and realized the final vote must lie there.

Odin looked at them all, then said, "Peace."

Thor turned to Odin. "You won't go to war?"

Odin nodded glumly. "Not until we've tested the prophesy."

"And if the giants attack us in the meantime?"

"Then you'll have your wish, my son." Odin looked at Joshua, Toby, and Yutang. "But as for what we should do with these boys—"

Loki said, "Send each to a different land, Brother. You'll know who we needed when one brings back the hammer."

Odin gave a grim smile of satisfaction. "Trust you to find a solution, Loki."

Thor laughed and clapped Loki on the back,

sending him staggering several steps forward. "That's what you're good at!"

Joshua said, "Where do you want to send us?"

"The giants did this," said Thor. "I'll take a boy to Jotunheim and prove it!"

Odin nodded. "Which one?"

Thor turned toward Toby, Joshua, and Yutang. Yutang wanted to ask if it was possible to go to any of these lands without flying in Thor's chariot. Toby may have wondered something similar, because he did not volunteer.

"I'll go," said Joshua.

Thor grinned. "We'll see if you're good with giant animals, lad!"

Freyr said, "The dwarves who made the hammer might've taken it back. I'll go with a boy to Nidavellir and ask them."

Odin shook his head. "Your nature makes you trusting, Freyr. To that dark place, we should send someone who trusts no one." He turned to Tyr, who was petting Lincoln as the dog sniffed his boots. "You, Tyr."

Tyr nodded and kept petting Lincoln.

"And for company…," Odin began.

Yutang started to step forward, but before he could, Toby said, "Take me."

"Very well," Odin agreed.

Loki said, "The elves might have their reasons for taking the hammer."

Freyr nodded. "Then I'll go to Alfheim."

Odin shook his head. "We should send them an envoy who sees subtle patterns in all things." He looked at Loki.

"But I'm busy—" Loki began.

"Too busy to find the hammer that keeps us all safe?"

"No." Loki sighed. "Never that busy." He smiled at Yutang. "This should be amusing."

Freyja said, "The end of all nine worlds may be approaching, and you think this could be amusing?"

Loki nodded. "People are at their best and their worst when disaster's near. Extremes are always amusing."

The end of all nine worlds? Yutang thought of his mother and father working in their shop. He saw Joshua and Toby hesitate at Freyja's words and knew they were thinking of people they loved. He wondered if the *Basset*'s crew had known so much was at stake, then realized it did not matter. The *Basset* had gotten the boys here. The rest was up to them.

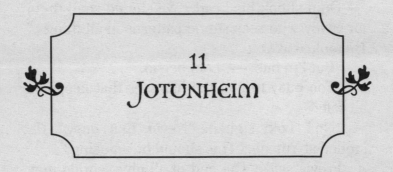

11
JOTUNHEIM

High above a wide, dark ocean, Joshua rode in Thor's chariot with the thunder god at the reins. Beside him, Lincoln stood with his front paws over the side of the chariot. Joshua squinted into a bitterly cold wind and shivered. He could have sat on the floor so the chariot's low wall would shield him. But he liked the cold wind lashing at his skin and the bright sun glaring down as the waters rolled by far beneath them. How could he have thought this was a dream? He'd never been so awake in his life!

He laughed. Thor glanced at him. "What's funny?"

"I thought this wasn't real at first."

"What?"

"All of this. The *Basset,* Asgard, you—"

Thor let loose his deep, sidesplitting laugh. "Me, not real? That *is* funny!"

It seemed funny now. Thor smelled of wood smoke and sweat. The goats had a musky odor like long-haired sheep. The wooden chariot was nicked and scarred from hard use. The cold wind flicked a strand of slobber away from Lincoln's jaws. If this was not real, the word *real* had no useful meaning.

Joshua said, "Who was that woman you kissed when we left? The one with the little girl?"

"The most beautiful woman in nine worlds?" Thor smiled, looking almost gentle for the first time since Joshua had met him. "My wife, Sif. The girl's our daughter, Thrud."

Joshua didn't know who the most beautiful woman in nine worlds might be. He thought Freyja was the most beautiful woman in Asgard, but he wasn't going to argue with the god of thunder. "Her hair looked like gold."

"It is gold."

"Like the metal?"

"Exactly like the metal. It is the metal."

Joshua squinted at Thor. Knowing this place was real did not mean he had to believe everything he heard. "She was born with hair made of gold?"

"No," Thor said with a chuckle. "That was one

of Loki's better tricks. Sif had the most beautiful hair, like a field of wheat on a sunny afternoon. One night, while she slept, Loki cut it all off."

"You thought that was *funny*?"

Thor shook his head. "I was furious. Loki does things he thinks are funny and doesn't see that people may be hurt. We told him to fix what he'd done or leave Asgard forever. So he went to the dwarves and came back with a wig made from strands of gold. When Sif put it on, it grew onto her head, every bit as beautiful as the hair Loki had cut."

"So you forgave him? Just like that?"

"He didn't just bring the wig for Sif. He had the dwarves make five other treasures." Thor ticked them off on the fingers of his left hand. "My hammer, Mjollnir. Odin's spear, Gungnir, which never misses. Odin's golden armband, Draupnir—every ninth night, it makes eight gold bands as large as itself. Freyr's ship, *Skidbladnir.* And Freyr's golden boar, named Gullinbursti. It can carry its rider anywhere, faster than any horse."

Something about Thor's simple way of telling about these things made Joshua believe him. They rode on in silence for a few minutes. Then Joshua thought of something else that had confused him. "Loki called Odin 'brother.' But he doesn't look anything like him."

"Loki is Odin's foster brother. He was born in Jotunheim, but he likes Asgard better. Among giants, he's a dwarf. Among us, he's a giant. When he behaves himself, I love him like a brother. When he plays one of his tricks, I hate him as much as I hate any giant. I have to remind myself that Loki makes himself useful."

"How?"

Thor scratched his bearded chin and watched the goats. Joshua thought he wouldn't answer, but then Thor said, "In the war between the Aesir and the Vanir, Asgard's wall was shattered. A stranger came to us and said that he and his horse could rebuild it in six months. All he asked in return was to marry Freyja and have the sun and the moon for wedding presents. If he failed to place the last stone by the last day of the sixth month, he would leave without any payment. We knew that building a stone wall around all of Asgard so quickly was impossible. But Loki pointed out that if we agreed, the stranger would work for free for six months, and we could finish the work easily after he failed. So we all agreed, even Freyja."

Seeing Thor shake his head, Joshua said, "My grandma said never bet on a sure thing, because the sure thing is that the person who made the bet knows how to win it."

"A shame she wasn't there to advise us. We

watched the stranger and his horse work night and day for month after month, the horse hauling the stones and the stranger putting them in place. The wall rose higher, stone after stone. We saw that the stranger would do what he had said."

Thor shook his head glumly. "And in that time, we got to know him. Not who he was, but what he was like. He was miserly and cruel. He only smiled when he told us about his plan to take Freyja and the sun and the moon away from us and hide them where only he could enjoy their company. We knew Freyja would suffer with such a husband, and we would suffer without the sun in daytime or the moon at night. The crops would fail. The snow would never melt. It would be the cold darkness of Fimbulvetr. We knew that we had been fools."

Joshua said, "What's Fimbulvetr?"

"The long winter that comes before Ragnarok." Thor grinned. "Now you want to know what Ragnarok is?"

Joshua nodded.

"It's the final battle, when Fenrir the great wolf and Jormungand the Midgard Serpent break free of their prisons, and Surt leads his demons from Muspellheim, the land of fire. All the nine worlds will be destroyed." Thor laughed.

"Now you want to know about Fenrir and Jormungand and Surt."

"Freyja said the end of the nine worlds may be approaching."

"Ragnarok comes during a time of war. But there's no way to know which war."

"But—"

Thor laughed. "There's barely time to finish this story. Hold your questions till later. That's Jotunheim." He pointed ahead at a green strip of woodland on the horizon.

"Now," Thor resumed, "no one knew what to do about the stranger, but we knew who had encouraged us to accept his terms. We went to Loki and told him this was his fault. He said the stranger could never finish the wall on time without his horse. So Loki turned himself into a mare—" Thor laughed louder than before. "If you could see your face, lad!"

As Joshua closed his mouth, Thor said, "Why do you think he's called Shapechanger if— Oh, right. I forget how little you know about us."

"Loki can turn into things? This isn't just a story?"

"All I say is true, lad. Loki says I don't have the wit to lie, and he may be right. It's hard enough dealing with what's true."

"So what did Loki do?"

Thor grinned. "On the morning of the last day, the stranger's horse spied a young mare in the woods. The horse chased the mare, and the stranger chased his horse. All day long, he hunted for his horse instead of working on the wall. When night came, the horse returned, too late." Thor nodded in satisfaction. "So Asgard's wall was built for free, thanks to Loki."

Then Thor laughed, perhaps his deepest laugh yet. "Loki stayed away from Asgard for months. When he came back, he brought a young horse with eight legs that he gave to Odin. It's called Sleipnir. There's no faster animal anywhere."

"You said Freyr's boar was faster than any horse."

"Huh." Thor scratched his beard. "We'll never know. I think Freyr is too wise to race Odin."

"You could say that the boar is faster than any four-legged animal."

"Huh!" Thor grinned. "I'm no storyteller, but you should be one!" He pointed downward. "Utgard. The largest city in Jotunheim."

At first, Joshua thought Utgard looked like a farm town of huts built inside a stone wall and surrounded by fields and bushes. But as the chariot descended, he saw that the bushes were actually towering trees and the stone wall was

built from giant boulders. The logs in the buildings' roofs must have been cut from trees as big
as those along the California coast, sequoias so
huge you could drive a horse and carriage into a
tunnel cut through one.

The town and its surrounding farms filled a
large valley. Utgard's roads were not paved, and
its people only built with logs and stones and
thatch, but Utgard sprawled over so much land
that it had to be as large as San Francisco, or
much larger. The smallest hut within its walls
was as large as Odin's great hall.

Giants went about their business, working
the fields or walking the streets or bustling
through a huge square where stalls and wagons
had been set up as a market. They varied wildly
in size. Some of the smaller ones, which Joshua
had thought were children, were adults half
again as tall as a tall human. Some of the larger
ones were children who stood several times as
tall as any human. The very largest were clearly
adults, and they were as tall as oak trees. Joshua
understood why Loki might prefer to live elsewhere.

The giants turned their faces up as the chariot passed over them. They pointed and shouted
things, but their words were lost in the wind as
the goats flew on. Joshua said, "They seem
awfully excited."

Thor grinned. "Of course. The god of thunder comes to visit them."

"Will we go to their king?"

"After we visit my first wife."

"Your first wife's here? In Jotunheim?"

Thor nodded and smiled.

"She's a giant?"

Thor nodded again.

"I thought you wanted to go to war with the giants!"

"Skrymir, their king, wants to conquer us. I hate him and his followers. But I could never hate Jarnsaxa or my sons."

"You have giant children?"

"Modi and Magni. They're half the reason why I must find Mjollnir. They should have the hammer after me." Thor drew on the reins, calling, "Ho, Tanngnost! Ho, Tanngrisni! You know this place!"

The goats flew downward as if racing down an imaginary hill. They headed toward a cottage by a field that lay far outside Utgard's enormous walls. Joshua thought it looked like a pretty little farm. Then he reminded himself that "little" was relative as they came to a stop on the lawn in front of a stone cottage as big as the largest barn he had ever seen on Earth.

Two red-haired boys ran laughing from the cottage to meet them. A pale-haired woman with a worried smile followed close behind. The boys looked about Joshua's age, though they were a head taller than Thor. The woman was another head taller than them. The boys wore blue and red wool tunics, dark trousers, and brown leather boots. The woman wore a red wool dress and brown boots like the ones the boys wore. Though the woman and the boys seemed friendly, Joshua was glad that they carried no weapons.

"Father!" the boys cried as Thor jumped to the ground. He caught them each in a fierce hug that lifted them off their feet. The giant woman watched, smiling. Thor turned to her with his arms spread wide. Her hug lifted the thunder god high into the air before she set him down again.

"Come on, Lincoln." Joshua stepped down, and Lincoln stayed close to him. He took a quick look around the farmstead. In the nearest field, he saw his first giant animal clearly. It was an ox, three times as tall as any he had seen, and its skin was dark blue.

"Modi," Thor said, nodding at the boy in the blue tunic, "Magni," nodding at the boy in the red, "and Jarnsaxa," nodding at the woman. "This is Joshua. He came from Midgard to find my hammer."

Jarnsaxa stared at Thor. "It's gone?"

"Who took it?" asked Modi.

"Ah, son." Thor reached up to scratch the giant boy's head as if their heights were reversed. "If I knew that, I wouldn't be here." He added, "We'll get it back," so confidently that Joshua felt as if he might really be the one who would succeed.

Jarnsaxa turned to Joshua. "Then you're especially welcome to our home. Come, you must be hungry and thirsty. I baked bread."

He hadn't thought he was hungry, but it had been a long time since his breakfast with the Carters. "Thank you."

"And there's cheese!" said Magni, rubbing his stomach.

"And peach cider!" added Modi. "I could drink a barrel."

"Hah!" said Magni, shoving Modi. "I could drink two!"

"Growing boys." Jarnsaxa smiled at Thor. As they walked toward the cottage, she said, "This isn't a good time for Aesir to visit Jotunheim."

"When is?" said Thor.

Modi said, "I never met anyone from Midgard."

"Then we're even," said Joshua. "I never met anyone from Jotunheim."

"Jotunheim's boring," said Magni. "There's mostly farming."

"We might go to war," said Modi hopefully.

"What's that?" asked Thor.

Jarnsaxa frowned. "Eat. Then talk about rumors."

Thor squinted at her. "Rumors that this is a good time to attack Asgard?"

Jarnsaxa nodded and went into the cabin.

The inside was dark and cool. It looked like a cottage built twice as large as it should be. The furniture was simple and old: wooden benches and stools, a rocking chair, and a kitchen table. An oven was built into the stone fireplace. The air smelled of baked bread and cut flowers. There were curtains over the windows, and the wooden floor was scrubbed clean. Huge wooden swords and a leather ball half as large as Joshua lay near the door.

Joshua felt a bit disappointed. There weren't any human heads on the walls or piles of gnawed bones on the floor. Then he saw a mountain lion lying on a cushion by a window in the sun. He froze, then relaxed when Thor patted its enormous skull and said, "Hello, Boots." Lincoln growled at the big cat. When it hissed, Lincoln ran close to Joshua. The cat curled up and went back to sleep.

Joshua had to jump up to sit on a stool by the table. He didn't feel as silly when he saw Thor do the same. While Modi and Magni ran for pillows to prop their guests up higher, Jarnsaxa brought out two loaves of brown bread as large as cartwheels, a wedge of yellow cheese as large as a boulder, and cider in a wooden barrel as large as Joshua.

"If we'd known you were coming—" Jarnsaxa began.

"That looks great," Thor said, tearing off a piece of bread as big as his head and a piece of cheese to match.

"Help yourself," Jarnsaxa told Joshua, handing him cider in a mug that he had to hold in both hands.

The peach cider was cold and tart, the cheese was cool and sharp, and the bread was warm and chewy. He ate happily while Thor told Jarnsaxa and the twins that Sif was well and Thrud was as strong as a giant baby.

Then the ground shook with a sound like a thunderstorm rolling toward them. Joshua glanced at the god in charge of thunder and saw Thor was as surprised as he was. Magni ran to the door as the ground continued to shake and called, "Company!"

Thor looked at Jarnsaxa. She shook her head, saying, "I'm not expecting anyone."

"It's the king!" Modi called.

As Thor and Jarnsaxa exchanged another look, a shadow fell over the hut. The mountain lion opened its eyes, looked around with something like disappointment, then went back to sleep. Joshua jumped down and followed Thor to the door.

The cottage had been in a plain, but now it was next to a snow-covered hill. Then Joshua saw that the hill was covered in green and brown wool, not grass and earth. The white at its top was hair and a beard, not snow. Two caves were nostrils. Eyes like charcoal peered at him. A mouth opened, showing teeth like a row of tombstones.

"Where is the thief?" Skrymir said, so loudly that Joshua clapped his hands over his ears and Lincoln hid at the back of the room.

Thor stepped outside. "That's what I've come to learn, Skrymir!"

Skrymir said, "You came here to learn where you are?" Then he laughed, rumbling like an avalanche. "Your sense of humor grows, little thief!"

"Thief? Me?" Thor put his hands on his hips. "You think I stole my own hammer?"

Skrymir shook his head. Flakes of dandruff fell, as large as playing cards. "You stole my crown!"

Thor stared up at the giant. "You think *I* stole your crown?"

Skrymir thundered, "I know you did!"

"Why would I?"

"For its jewels. For the insult to Jotunheim. Because you haven't found the traitor who stole your hammer, so you blamed me. If you don't know why you did it, how could I tell you?"

"A traitor? In Asgard? Who would—?" Thor's voice turned cold and bitter. "Loki!"

"You blame my misbegotten son?" Skrymir said, laughing like a tornado whirling around Jarnsaxa's cottage. "Well, little Loki's clever enough to escape you, I'm sure. Now return my crown!"

"I didn't take it!"

"I saw you, thunder god! Not ten minutes before you flaunted yourself by flying over my capitol—"

Joshua shouted, "Thor couldn't have stolen it! We just came from Asgard!"

Skrymir's black eyes flicked to Joshua, then back to Thor. "The boy's lies cannot save you. You may've escaped me before." Skrymir reached down and caught Thor like a doll in his huge fist. "You can't escape me now!"

"Joshua!" Thor called as he struggled in Skrymir's grip. "Get back to Valaskjalf! Tell Odin what's happened!"

Skrymir grinned. "Why bother? I've ordered my armies to march on Asgard. He'll know soon enough."

Joshua glanced at Jarnsaxa. "Go!" she cried. "There's nothing you can do here!"

Joshua nodded and ran for the chariot with Lincoln at his side. A shadow came over him, and he knew that a giant hand was reaching for him. It clapped down over him like a cage.

Lincoln barked furiously from outside the giant's hand. Through the gaps between the fingers, Joshua could see Lincoln biting the giant, to no effect. "Get back!" Joshua ordered, but for the first time in years, the dog disobeyed him. Joshua wondered if he could wriggle through, but feared that would only make the giant clench his fist.

"What are you, little dark boy?" Skrymir asked. "If I close my hand, will you break like a human?"

"Leave him!" Thor called. "He's no threat—"

True, Joshua thought in despair, *I'm nothing that a giant would fear. Unless*— "No, Thor! We should tell him! Not even Skrymir deserves my fate!"

"Tell him nothing!" Thor shouted.

"Tell me what?" Skrymir roared.

"What I am," Joshua said. "What'll happen to you if—"

"If?" Skrymir asked. "Tell me, or I'll squash you!"

"Then it'll be too late for sure!"

"Too late for what?"

"To save you!"

Skrymir gawked at him, then laughed. "Why would you save me?"

"Because I was a giant, like you!" Joshua said. "Though not so small. Until *it* happened."

Skrymir's smile had gone. "Until what happened?"

"I caught a little brown man a month ago. He told me he had been a giant, but he caught the shrinking disease." Joshua stopped to study Skrymir's face, and saw a trace of doubt there. "He said the longer we were touching, the more sure I was to catch it. Oh, if I'd only believed him!"

"Why?" Skrymir demanded.

"I carried him home and put him in a cage. He escaped a few days later. He had shrunk so small that he slipped between the bars."

The hand drew back as if it had been about to close on a burning coal. Skrymir said, "I have Thor. I don't need a little brown boy."

"Go, Joshua!" Thor called. "Before he changes his mind!"

Joshua hesitated, then said, "Thor was traveling with me because he has the shrinking disease, too."

"You lie!" Skrymir said, with more doubt in his voice.

"Look at him! He must be six inches shorter than the last time you saw him!"

Skrymir opened his hand like a man bit by a mosquito, dropping Thor from where he held him so high in the air. Joshua stared, horrified, afraid that he had only succeeded in getting the thunder god killed. Thor crashed through the top of a maple tree, caught himself in its lower branches, then dropped to the ground and landed heavily on his feet.

Skrymir said, "You don't have your hammer, little thief. You can't stop my armies. I don't care whether you're shrinking or not. Go back to Asgard and watch my army crush you!" He turned and strode away.

Jarnsaxa and the twins ran to Thor. He embraced them quickly, then said, "I must go. Will you be safe?"

Jarnsaxa grinned at Joshua. "Who will bother us while we have the shrinking disease?"

Thor smiled and ran for the chariot with Joshua and Lincoln. Jarnsaxa called, "Luck be with you!" as they scrambled into it. Thor grabbed the reins, called, "And with you!" then shouted, "Ho, Tanngrisni! Ho, Tanngnost! To Odin's hall in Asgard."

The goats leaped, the chariot lurched, and then they were flying high and fast, back the way they had come. Joshua glanced behind them.

Jarnsaxa and the twins were waving, so he waved back.

Thor glanced at him. "Were you really a giant?"

Joshua shook his head.

Thor exhaled in relief, then said, "I didn't think so."

And they flew on toward Asgard.

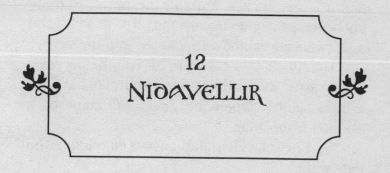

12
NIÐAVELLIR

In a land filled with magic, Toby thought, there must some way to help his family. So what if the crew of the *Basset* weren't leprechauns with treasure? He was going to see dwarves who made magical things from gold! And the Aesir must be planning to reward whoever helped them. All he had to do was to make sure that that was him. He grinned, sure of one thing: If he kept his eyes open, he would see his chance, sooner or later.

Perhaps his chance was already beneath him. Toby and Tyr rode away from Asgard on the back of Sleipnir, Odin's eight-legged gray horse. If Toby could take Sleipnir to San Francisco, people would happily pay a nickel to see such a sight.

Tyr raced Sleipnir up to a gate made all of gold. In front of it, a brown-bearded guard in a horned helmet stood with a spear in one hand and a large, curved horn in the other. Nothing lay beyond the gate except the edge of a cliff and a shimmering rainbow that arced into the sky.

"Heimdall!" Tyr called in his rough, low voice as he raised the leather-bound stump of his right arm in salute. "Open the gates! We come on a mission from Odin!"

"So I heard," Heimdall answered, pulling the gate wide.

"Uh, Tyr?" Toby asked as the dark-haired Aesir shook Sleipnir's reins. "We're not going over that cliff?"

"Of course not."

"Good." Toby relaxed.

Tyr said, "We're going over that rainbow."

"You can't—" Toby began, too late.

"Ho, Sleipnir!" Tyr cried. The gray horse's eight legs churned beneath them, carrying them swiftly toward the cliff's edge.

"Good luck!" Heimdall called, closing the gate behind them.

"We may need more than that," Tyr answered—not an answer that Toby wanted to hear.

Beyond the cliff, the sky fell away. Clouds floated far beneath them. As Sleipnir threw himself over the edge, Toby swallowed and closed his eyes. He wondered if he and Tyr and Sleipnir would fall forever through space, or if there was firm ground somewhere below, where they would crash in an hour or so.

It felt as though they were climbing. Maybe, he thought, they had died and their souls were rising to heaven. He opened his eyes, half expecting to see his body broken on rocks below him. Instead, he saw Sleipnir running up the rainbow into the bright blue sky.

He could see through the brilliant bands of color to the clouds drifting by beneath them. The sight made his stomach wobble. But Sleipnir's hooves clattered on the rainbow as if it were solid. If he didn't look down, Toby could imagine they were riding on solid ground. "This is that bridge!"

"Bifrost," said Tyr.

"I thought taking it was slower than taking the *Basset*."

"Not on Sleipnir. And where we're going, no ship can go: to Nidavellir, where Svartalfheim lies."

"Where dwarves live."

"And dark elves." Tyr spoke the last words as though he hated their feel in his mouth.

Toby frowned. Dwarves and elves were tiny, so they couldn't be much of a danger. Was Tyr worried because they would be outnumbered? Toby couldn't do anything about that, so he asked, "Why didn't Odin ride Sleepy over the rainbow to fetch us in the first place?"

"Freyja's prophecy."

When more explanation didn't come, Toby said, "You don't talk much, do you, Mr. Tyr?"

"No."

"Odin said we'd be told what we should know as we traveled."

Tyr sighed. "Yes."

"So why does the prophecy keep anyone else from fetching us?"

"The prophecy foretold that the *Basset* would find one to save Asgard this noon in San Francisco."

Toby grinned. "So we don't have anything to worry about."

"If the prophecy is true. And if you're the one. If it's one of your friends, you and I may have much to worry about."

Toby wondered why he had chosen to go with someone as glum as Tyr. Then he remembered how flying in Thor's chariot made him nauseous. And the more important factor: He had seen how the other Aesir treated Tyr with respect, even though he had only one hand.

"Well," Toby said, "at least we have a beautiful day for our worrying." He looked out—but not down—at the amazing view. The hills of Asgard fell far behind them, and harsh, rocky mountains rose from the clouds before them.

Tyr grunted.

Toby asked, "Did you lose your hand in a battle?"

"Hmm," said Tyr. "A battle of sorts."

"Do you think it might be important for me to know about it?"

Tyr gave Toby a smile, which was more frightening that his usual dour expression. "You remember the giant, Loki?"

"The tall man."

Tyr nodded. "Loki had a giant wife named Angrboda. They had three children, each a monster. First came Fenrir, a giant wolf. Then came Jormungand, a giant serpent. Third came Hel, who looks half like a living woman, half like a dead one."

Toby shuddered. If Tyr noticed, he did not stop his story. "Odin wondered what Loki's children would do. So he went to the Norns."

"Who?"

"Three sisters who can see the future. The Norns said Loki's children will join Surt, the fire demon. Together, they will attack Asgard at Ragnarok, the last battle, and all nine worlds will end. To delay that fatal day, Odin put Loki's children where they cannot harm us. He sent Hel to Niflheim, land of the dead. She rules there as their queen. Thor threw Jormungand into the ocean surrounding Midgard. Jormungand continued to grow there. Now his body encircles all of Midgard, and he sleeps with his tail between his teeth. But no one knew what to do with the great wolf."

"Fenrir."

"Yes. Odin had the dwarves forge a golden chain so thin that it looked like a baby could snap it. But it was not made from gold. It was made from a mountain's roots, a woman's beard, a fish's breath, a bird's spit, a bear's vigor, and the sound of a cat's footstep."

Toby laughed. "Who checked the ingredients?"

Tyr narrowed his eyes. "No Aesir could break it, not even Thor. So we took it to Fenrir and said we had a bet about whether he was strong enough to break it."

"He believed that?"

"He was suspicious. He said he wouldn't let the chain be wrapped around him unless one of us put a hand in his jaw until the chain was broken or removed."

"But you didn't plan to remove the chain!"

"No," said Tyr, sad and proud both at once.

Toby imagined Tyr putting his hand in a giant wolf's mouth, knowing he was about to lose it.

How could he have done it? But maybe something like that had happened when the machine had cut his own hand. Tyr had done it to keep Asgard safe. And Toby had done what he had to so his family would be safe.

Toby looked at his crippled hand. Maybe it wasn't something to be ashamed of. Maybe it was something to be proud of.

"Where's Fenrir now?"

"Chained far below the island of Lyngvi, until Ragnarok comes."

The rainbow ended in a bleak mountain range. Only a few shrubs and stunted trees dotted the cliffs. Toby took a quick look around, just in case a leprechaun had left some gold there, but saw none. He said, "Are there different rainbows to different places?"

"Follow a different color to different worlds." Tyr pointed at the six colors of the rainbow. "Blue for Asgard, green for Midgard, violet for both Nidavellir and Svartalfheim, where we have come. There are no bridges to the worlds of Hel's shadows or Surt's flames."

"Nidavellir and Svartalfheim count as separate worlds?"

"One is the land of dwarves, one of dark elves. Once they were truly separate worlds, but now the dark elves rule in both."

Sleipnir galloped off the rainbow onto a

narrow road carved along the side of the mountain. Toby sighed with relief. They might be in danger, but at least it was danger on solid ground. He said, "If there's a rainbow to the giants' land, couldn't they use it to attack Asgard?"

"They will, someday. That's why Heimdall stands guard. He sleeps less than a bird. He can hear grass growing and see an ant crawl thirty miles away. When an army comes, he will sound the horn Gjall, which can be heard throughout the nine worlds. Asgard will have some warning."

Sleipnir raced around the side of the mountain and halted. "Svartalfheim," Tyr said. "The city of the dark elves."

Toby looked ahead, expecting to see buildings and streets. All he saw was the mountainside. He looked suspiciously at Tyr. "There's nothing there."

Tyr pointed to a huge boulder. "That is the gate." He shouted, "Greetings from Asgard to Svartalfheim!"

Toby looked to see if someone was hiding in the rocks. Then the boulder rolled aside, more quietly than most doors. A cave lay before them. Its walls and roof were rough from nature's work, but its floor was as smooth as a city street. Along the roof, a line of dim, glowing lights proceeded deep into the earth.

Two soldiers in black armor stepped out. They were at least as tall as Toby and as broad as Thor. Their foreheads protruded far over their eyes, their noses protruded far over their mouths, and their muscular arms seemed as long as a gorilla's. One, who was female, carried a war ax. The other, male, carried a huge hammer.

"They're dwarves," Tyr said, and Toby realized that these dwarves were only short when they stood next to Aesir.

"Tyr Odinsson!" the dwarf woman called. "Do you bring work for our smiths?"

"No, Uni. Odin sends me as his envoy to the Dark Lady."

Uni's eyes opened till they were round as saucers, then closed again. "One moment." She turned to the male dwarf. "Durin. Tell the Dark Court that I bring visitors from Asgard."

"At once!" Durin ran into the cave.

"Now we may go more leisurely," Uni said. "Come."

Tyr swung down from the saddle, so Toby slid off the blanket that he had used for cushioning. Uni led them into the mouth of the cave, where six more dwarf soldiers waited. One, standing by an enormous iron lever, said, "Shall I close the way?"

Uni looked at the boulder, then shook her

head. "A work crew will be coming soon. Just keep a good watch."

They left Sleipnir in an alcove with hay and water, then headed on. The dim lights along the ceiling were glowing globes that bobbed in the air currents. They were so far apart that Toby, Tyr, and Uni had to walk through darkness each time they passed one.

At first, the lights revealed rough stone walls like a crude tunnel. But deeper in the earth, the cave changed. Toby gawked at curtains of white rock where stone appeared to have flowed like water and frozen in place, at stalactites hanging from the ceiling and stalagmites rising from the ground like enormous teeth, at columns thicker than any tree and curtains of stone as thin as lace.

Uni smiled at him. "Dwarf work is good, as you shall see. But it cannot compare to nature's."

As they continued, the cave twisted ahead of them. Tyr made the turn first, then stopped so abruptly that Toby bumped into him.

He looked into an enormous cavern. A large floating globe glowed within it like a small moon. But while the globe was amazing, what it lit was even more wonderful.

The path plunged down to a wide chasm. A stone bridge arced across the gap. On the other side, a city had been carved into the sides of the cavern from its roof to its distant floor. All around the large floating globe, people moved on a delicate spiderweb of stairs and bridges.

Toby's first thought was that Uni had been too modest. The city fit this place perfectly, as if nature had been waiting for the dwarves to finish her work. Even the bridge seemed as if it had always been a part of this place.

While he admired the view, someone called, "Make way!"

He glanced down. Two young dwarves staggered up the path, bent under the weight of a pointed golden pole as thick as a fence post and as long as two horses. A slender man, as tall as Tyr but as pale as snow, followed close behind. His eyes were silver. His ears came to points. The dwarves wore rough wool clothes, but the silver-eyed man was dressed in black clothes as light as silk, with red gems for buttons.

A bench had been carved into the wall of the cave, where people could rest. Uni and Tyr stepped beside it. Toby, wanting to keep looking at the city, jumped onto the bench.

Coming near, one of the dwarves stumbled under the weight of his burden. The silver-eyed man said, "Take care with Skrymir's toothpick, you fool!"

"That," Tyr told Toby, "is a dark elf."

"Are elves not wee folk?" Toby asked.

"None that I know of," Tyr said with his grim smile.

The two dwarves climbed onward. Uni nodded to them, her large brow furrowed in concern. Toby understood why a moment later. One of the young dwarves slipped to one knee and almost dropped his end of the giant's toothpick.

"Imbecile!" the elf cried from where he stood, only a step away from Toby. He lifted his arm, and a whip appeared in his fist.

An image flashed through Toby's mind of Beasley's men hitting O'Hara and breaking his sign. Without thinking, Toby caught the whip and pulled it from the elf's hand.

The elf whirled to face him and sniffed the air. "Human. What do you have to say for yourself?"

Toby looked at the whip in his hand and thought, *How much trouble have I gotten us in now?* Then he grinned at the elf and said, "Thank you?"

Uni made a sound that might have been a laugh. When Toby glanced at her, she covered her mouth and coughed.

"You will pay—" the elf began.

"For a gift?" said Tyr.

"Is he your servant?" the elf asked Tyr. "Or does he answer for his own actions?"

"I'm not—" Toby began.

"He travels with me," Tyr said. "We are

envoys from Asgard. What would the Dark Lady think of you for troubling her guests?"

The elf's pale skin grew paler. He snapped his fingers, and the whip disappeared from Toby's hand. "It was no gift," he said, then turned to the young dwarves. "Be more careful."

"Yes, sir," said the dwarf who had fallen. Both dwarves and the elf marched up and around the path.

"Will they be all right?" Toby asked.

"As much as anyone can be with dark elves for masters," Tyr said. "They're past the steep part."

Toby thought Uni was watching them, but she looked away as soon as he glanced toward her. He asked, "Why do they call them dark elves if they're so white? Because they live in caves?"

"Because that's the color of their deeds," said Tyr. "Among the light elves, there are those whose skin is as dark as your friend's."

Uni stepped closer to Toby. "Thank you. The boy who fell is my son."

"Oh," Toby said. "Is he a slave?"

"No!" Uni answered angrily.

Tyr said, "Toby's from Midgard, Uni Dvallins-dottir. He doesn't know your ways."

Uni's face softened. "We're not slaves, Toby of Midgard. We're servants. The dark elves give us work," she explained. Then her face hardened again. "Work under foul conditions for little reward."

"So refuse to do it," Toby said. "Until they make things better for you."

Her eyes widened again. "The elves would only bring trolls from the Iron Woods to work for them. We would starve!"

"Couldn't you get the trolls to refuse to work, too?"

"Trolls!" Uni spat. "They're our enemies!"

"Huh," said Toby. "Are they worse than these dark elves?"

Uni frowned at him. She opened her mouth to speak, then turned away. "Let's go on."

As they crossed the bridge to Svartalfheim, Durin marched toward them with six dwarf soldiers. Each carried a long pike. Durin raised his arm in a salute to Uni, then said, "You may return. The Lady sends this honor guard to escort her visitors."

Toby glanced at Tyr to see what that meant. Tyr shrugged. "We know the way."

Durin said, "You come as Asgard's envoy. This is only your due."

Uni frowned at Durin, then nodded. "Good luck with your mission, Tyr Odinsson and Toby of Midgard."

Toby said, "Thanks, Uni."

As Uni left, the seven dwarf soldiers surrounded Toby and Tyr. "This way," said Durin, taking the lead.

Durin walked more briskly than Uni, forcing Toby to hurry instead of gawk. Still, as they walked along a broad avenue cut into the cliff, he saw dark elves in luxurious clothing and dwarves dressed as soldiers and servants. The huge globe in the middle of the cavern lit the scene like a full moon. Little floating lights drifted just overhead along the street. Through open doors and windows, he saw more little lights bobbing. He heard music played by bands of dwarves with drums and fiddles. They passed dark elves drinking and dancing together, and he heard them laugh and joke.

"Is there a celebration tonight?" Toby asked.

"It's day," Durin said. "Every day is much like this."

The dwarf soldiers took them to a tall golden door covered with sculptures of dark elves hunting and fighting. A soldier opened it. Toby hesitated as a harsh light the color of blood spilled out, staining the stone street.

"If you please," Durin said.

Toby didn't please. But Tyr entered, so he followed.

The doors opened into a large room. All its walls were carved with statues of dark elves, looking exactly like the dark elves who sprawled on pillows around the room, eating fruit and meat from golden platters on low tables and drinking from golden goblets.

At the center of the room, the Dark Lady rose from her seat. She did not need an introduction—all the chatter and laughter and music in the room stopped when she stood. Her skin looked pink under the floating red lights, and so did her gown and her hair. She looked slender, strong, and beautiful. And she frightened Toby more than anyone he had ever seen.

He followed Tyr up to her and tried to keep his fear hidden.

"Tyr Odinsson," she said. "I had not thought to see you again so soon."

Tyr frowned. "It's been years."

"Not so long as that." She smiled as if she was about to offer a guest something to drink. "But your memory will improve after some time in my deepest, dankest dungeon. You do recognize the honor that I grant you and your companion? I would never give that cell to common thieves."

Durin's six soldiers aimed their pikes at Tyr and Toby. Tyr glanced at them, then held his arms out from his body to show that he had no weapons. "I'm here as Odin's envoy."

The Dark Lady gracefully waved her hand as if tossing away his objection. "The duties of an envoy will never protect a thief. Take them."

The dwarf soldiers moved closer. The tip of one pike brushed Toby's cheek, scratching it like a thorn.

"What has been stolen?" Tyr demanded.

The Dark Lady raised one eyebrow. "You take my necklace, then return ten minutes later and claim ignorance? I confess, I find that so curious that I shall ask you to tell me more, in five or ten years, when I care to visit your cell."

Tyr shouted, "Sleipnir! To me!"

The Dark Lady's mouth gaped in alarm. A worried murmur washed across all the assembled dark elves. Then the Dark Lady turned to Durin and said, "Is the entrance closed?"

"No, Lady. A work party—"

"Send your fastest soldier at once and close it!"

"I go!" Durin said, leaping away as he spoke.

Tyr picked up a low table and spun it around him, knocking away the pikes aimed at him and Toby. Then he threw the table at Durin. The dwarf jumped over it and ran out the door.

"Come!" Tyr said. He wrenched a pike from one dwarf soldier and used it like a staff to drive the other soldiers back. Toby ran after him to the Dark Lady's door. The dark elves scurried out of their way, and Toby thought for a moment that he and Tyr could escape.

In the street, they hesitated only long enough

to look both ways. More dwarf soldiers ran
toward them from the heart of the city. On the
path to the entrance, Durin was already over the
bridge and racing up the steep path.

Toby ran with all his might to escape Svartalfheim. He tried not to remember that it was
uphill all the way. He heard dwarf soldiers chasing them and knew that they climbed this path
every day. Ahead of him, he saw that Tyr ran as
quickly as he—and no faster.

"Leave me behind!" Toby shouted.

"You may be Asgard's savior!" Tyr answered.
"And even if you aren't, I'll never leave a companion behind!"

Toby's heart beat madly in his chest, and his
lungs pumped desperately for oxygen as he
began to run up the bridge. Dwarf soldiers ran so
close behind him that he could hear their breathing. He knew he could not make it. He wanted to
drop and let the soldiers take him, but he was
afraid Tyr would turn back to save him. Then
they would both be prisoners.

Above them, Durin approached the top of the
long, steep climb out of the cavern. Then the
dwarf threw himself onto a stone bench as Sleipnir charged by.

The stallion raced down to them. His eight
hooves ringing on the stone sounded like a cavalry troop attacking. Toby heard dwarf soldiers

curse and Tyr laugh grimly. When Sleipnir reached them, he rose up on his four rear legs, kicking his front four at the soldiers. Tyr leaped onto Sleipnir's broad back, caught Toby as he scrambled up after him, and called, "Hi-yo, Sleipnir! Away!" The stallion wheeled and bolted back the way they had come, galloping easily across the long bridge and up the steep incline.

Toby heaved a sigh of relief. They had failed to find the hammer, but he and Tyr would get back. Then he remembered Durin. The dwarf was nowhere in sight. He asked, "If they close the entrance—"

"Not even Sleipnir can carry us out," Tyr said.

They both had to stoop at the top of the path where the cavern ended and the long, dark cave began. Sleipnir ran so fast that the stretches of light and darkness pulsed by. Far ahead lay the brightness of day. Toby feared that Durin had made it to the cave's mouth, then saw the dwarf speeding from one patch of shadow to the next.

Toby grinned as Sleipnir flew past Durin, and shouted, "Slowpoke!"

The daylight grew brighter. He could see the six soldiers on guard duty turning to stare at them. They must think a whirlwind was roaring from the heart of the earth. Maybe they were right, he thought. They couldn't stand before Sleipnir.

Then Durin's voice boomed up from the cave. "Close the way! The Lady commands it!"

"Faster!" Toby called to Sleipnir.

A soldier grabbed the huge iron lever as Sleipnir approached.

"Odin needs us now!" Tyr called to the horse.

Toby would not have thought it possible, but the eight legs quickened their pace. Sleipnir's muscles rippled and his breath grew loud and harsh. He stroked the horse's side, and his fingers came away wet with sweat. He knew that Sleipnir would carry them free, that nothing could stop them now. As the stallion leaped forward, the sunlight seemed so bright that Toby could not see. He smelled pine trees and knew he would be back in the outer world in in seconds—

And the huge boulder rolled from the side of the mountain to seal the way. Sleipnir halted so abruptly that he had to rear up on his hind legs to keep from hitting the boulder. Toby clung desperately to the back of the saddle as Sleipnir whirled again.

Uni ran from the iron lever. Six more dwarf soldiers marched from the guard station with pikes, axes, and warhammers raised. Durin, breathing heavily, ran out of the shadows and shouted, "They stole the Lady's necklace!"

Far in the distance, Toby could hear the low

rumble of more soldiers running up from Svartalfheim. "What can we do?" he whispered.

"When there's nothing to be won by fighting,"
Tyr said, "surrender." He called, "Tell the Lady
that the thief only looked like me. If—"

"She has made up her mind," Durin said. "All
you can do is hope she changes it someday. Our
cells are not comfortable places to spend the rest
of your lives." He gestured toward the other
dwarves. "Take them."

The soldiers started walking toward them.
Toby looked at Tyr, wondering whether they
should jump down or let the dwarves drag them.

Then Uni said, "Did I tell anyone to arrest
them?"

Durin gawked at her. "The Lady com-
manded—"

"The Lady," Uni said, "has refused to raise
our pay every time we asked her."

The other dwarves stopped to stare at her.

Uni continued, "If her wishes were not
carried out so quickly or so well, she might re-
consider."

Durin began, "But she—"

"Tyr Odinsson's no thief," Uni cut in. "And
Toby of Midgard has a hero's heart. Should we
give them to the Dark Lady?"

A slow smile grew on Durin's face. "The run
from her hall to here takes time, if you pace

yourself...."

Uni nodded. "Enough time that we wouldn't have known to close the way..."

She looked at the soldier closest to the iron lever. He laughed and pushed the lever back. The great boulder rolled away, revealing sunlight and freedom.

Uni finished her sentence. "...and her visitors would've easily sped past us."

Toby grinned at her, then wondered why Tyr waited, looking at the seven dwarves as the tramping of the approaching soldiers grew louder.

Tyr said, "My thanks, Uni Dvallinsdottir. It seems I didn't know your ways, either."

"Go!" Durin said. "The Lady plans to help the giants attack Asgard if her necklace isn't returned."

Uni added, "I may convince dwarves and trolls not to fight for her. But there's still her dark elf cavalry."

Tyr nodded. He turned Sleipnir away from the dwarves and their cave, and cried, "Run, Sleipnir, as you've never run before!"

And as Sleipnir carried them away, Toby's fears for Asgard were lightened by Uni's words "a hero's heart." He prayed that he could find Thor's hammer, because he knew he already had his reward.

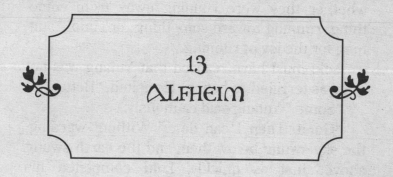

13
ALFHEIM

Yutang never thought that he would wish to be on Thor's chariot. But that would have been far better than riding through the air on Loki's back while the Trickster's flying boots carried them both. Loki leaned into the wind like a skater or a skier. If Yutang closed his eyes, he could pretend that they were racing downhill or across a frozen lake. But he was too terrified to close his eyes— Loki had started the flight by letting go of one of Yutang's legs, then laughing when Yutang gasped. And he was too fascinated as well.

Lush green plains rippled far below them. A wide river rolled toward a distant forest that filled the horizon. A flock of geese flew in a vee with them for several minutes, then seemed to decide that Loki and Yutang looked too odd in their formation and veered away. A herd of shaggy brown deer ran across the plain. Yutang couldn't see whether they were running away from something, running toward something, or simply running for the joy of running.

Loki must have realized that Yutang was not quite as terrified as before. He asked, "Better?"

"Some," Yutang said cautiously.

"Good. Then I can do..." Without warning, the sky swung below them and the earth swung above. Just as quickly, Loki completed his overhead loop and put the sky and the earth back where Yutang liked them. "...this," Loki finished.

Yutang said, "Yes, if you want me to throw up on you."

Loki sighed and flew onward, keeping them perfectly level. "Someday I'll think of a joke that can't turn to bite me. Do you know any amusing stories?"

"I'm sorry. No."

"Useless boy," Loki said, in the mild way anyone else would say, "I'm bored." Then he added hopefully, "Unless you find the hammer. Do you think you might?"

Yutang hoped he would and feared he couldn't. "I do not know."

"I could drop you," Loki offered. "If you're the promised one, something might save you. Say, a giant bird swooping down to catch you. Or maybe you'd land in thick bushes. What do you say?"

Yutang swallowed and wished again that he had gone with Thor. "Do you think the prophecy will come true no matter what? That it is fate?"

Loki sighed and shook his head. "We have minds, so we must have choice. If I didn't think so, I'd be home in Asgard with Sigyn, my wife. And if I had to be carting some boy on my back, I'd choose one of our sons, Vali or Narvi, even if their giant blood makes them larger than you."

"Then you care how this ends."

Loki laughed. "Only out of self-interest, boy. Watching the worlds end would be grand. But things would be so dull afterward."

"You're sure the worlds end if the hammer isn't found?"

Loki nodded. "If I were Surt—which is to say, humorless, stupid, ugly, and fixed on one thing, the destruction of Asgard—and I knew Thor's hammer was missing, I would come from Muspellheim with all my fire demons. I would invite Hel to lead her army of the dead, and the Dark Lady to bring her dwarves and dark elves, and Skrymir to call upon his giants. I would tell Fenrir and Jormungand that Ragnarok had come at last, so they would burst their bonds to join me. Before that force, Asgard and her allies would fall. Surt and his forces would be destroyed, too.

Being humorless, stupid, and ugly, that would be the best thing that could happen to them. But not to me. There's too much amusement in life to let it go so easily."

Another advantage to traveling with Thor, Yutang thought, was that anyone could understand the way the thunder god thought. Seeing a cluster of wooden buildings along the river, he changed the subject. "What's that?"

"Vanaheim, home of the Vanir."

"But Freyr and Freyja live in Asgard now."

"As do Heimdall and Njord the sea lord and Kvasir the Wise. When the war between the Aesir and the Vanir ended, some Aesir were sent to live in Vanaheim, and some Vanir were sent to Asgard."

Yutang thought about leaving his home after a war to live with the people who had killed his friends, family, or neighbors. "I would hate that."

Loki shrugged. "Vanaheim hasn't recovered from the war. It's awfully boring. The Vanir who came to Asgard had the better part of the bargain."

The city disappeared behind them as the plain gave way to broad woodland. Yutang asked, "How far to Alfheim?"

"We're there," Loki answered.

Yutang craned his neck to look around. He

saw nothing but forest in every direction. "I cannot see it. Because of the trees."

"Alfheim *is* the trees." Loki swooped down toward a tall oak that towered above all the others. "It's everything that grows here. And nothing else."

Loki landed in a glade. Yutang jumped down, glad to be on the ground again. The place was beautiful and quiet. Small blue flowers dotted the grass. In Alfheim, did flowers grow in winter? Or was it somehow spring here? The air was cool, but not as cool as Asgard's.

Yutang opened his jacket as he studied the glade. He saw no sign that any person had ever been here before. Had Loki chosen this place to abandon him? He didn't know if he could find his way out of the wood, let alone back to Asgard.

Loki looked at his face and laughed at his dismay. "What did you expect? This place is as boring as Vanaheim."

A gentle, high-pitched voice came from behind them. "So you bring us excitement, Loki Skytraveler?"

Yutang spun around. He saw no one in the bushes or in the shadows under the trees. Then he noticed Loki looking up. Yutang tilted his head back and stared.

A slender woman and a slender man sat

comfortably on a high branch, dangling their feet beneath them. They wore clothes the color of young oak leaves: tunics, tight leggings, and low boots, all made of some cloth as light as linen or silk. Their eyes and their skin were as pale as the moon. Their ears came to points. His hair was dark green; hers, dark purple.

"I bring you a boy," said Loki. "He may help us all. I bring a question, too."

The elves laughed. "You *are* a question, Skytraveler. The little giant whose bad instincts sometimes lead to good deeds."

Loki bowed. "Birdsong and Brook, I give you Lin Yutang of Midgard."

The elves smiled coolly. "Welcome, Linyutang. Treat this place well, and it will do the same for you."

Wondering which was Birdsong and which was Brook, Yutang imitated Loki's bow. "Thank you." He couldn't tell whether they had both spoken so far, or if only one of them had. Their expressions changed constantly, like clouds in the wind, but the emotions they showed were all merely degrees of amusement. No wonder Odin had sent Loki to them.

"What is your question, Skytraveler?"

"Where is Thor's hammer?"

The elves tittered like birds. "A surprisingly simple question from you, Skytraveler."

Loki bowed again. "I'd be grateful for a surprisingly simple answer."

"We shall look into this. Please, rest here."

"Thank you."

The elves fell backward off the branch. Yutang had a moment to fear they would be hurt, or worse. But as they fell, they became eagles, beat their wings mightily, and flew away.

Yutang looked at Loki, who shrugged. "Elves do that. They think it's impressive."

"It is."

"Did I say it wasn't?" Loki shrank without warning, his skin growing darker and sprouting feathers, his bones and muscles twisting, his clothes dissolving. A crow stood where Loki had been. It cocked its head and said, "But it's not *that* impressive."

Yutang laughed. "Can everyone in these lands turn into something else?"

The crow shook its head. "The Aesir don't. The secret's known to some giants, most elves, and several Vanir, like Freyja. It can be—" The crow lifted its wings in a shrug.

"Amusing?" Yutang suggested. He was beginning to understand how Loki thought.

"Yes. What's truly impressive is behind you."

Yutang whirled. In the middle of the glade, where there had only been grass and flowers, vines were weaving themselves into two chairs and a small table.

"Shall we?" Looking his tall, sharp-faced self again, Loki waved Yutang toward the table.

Yutang tried to look as though furniture grew every day in his family's workshop. He followed Loki to the table. They waited and watched the vines weave in and out of each other to become a surface like wicker.

Then Loki sat, so Yutang did, too. The chair felt comfortable at first, and it became more comfortable the longer he sat in it. It slowly shaped itself to fit his body. The sensation was odd. Chairs shouldn't do that. Yet he liked the feeling of the vines massaging his back.

He was watching the table to see if food and drink would grow out of it when Brook and Birdsong returned. "We have no answer for you yet, Skytraveler and Linyutang. But we have refreshment."

They carried two dark wooden trays. Each held three covered pottery bowls painted with scenes of animals in the woods. Though the bowls were beautiful, they looked perfectly ordinary. Yutang found that comforting, until he thought that in a place of magic, anything could be inside them.

He said, "Thank you," as the elves set the table with napkins, wooden spoons, and the six bowls. The elves removed the covers. The contents looked ordinary, too, but delicious. The two smallest bowls held grape juice. Two larger bowls held stew. One of the largest bowls held rolls of brown bread. The other held fruits that he had never expected to see in wintertime: tangerines, strawberries, and bananas.

"Enjoy. You shall have an answer soon." The elves smiled, turned themselves into foxes, and ran into the woods.

Loki said softly, "Isn't nearly as impressive if you do it all the time." He ate a spoonful of stew, said more loudly, "This is good!" and began shoveling food into his mouth as though he were starving.

Yutang saw that the stew had cubes of meat mixed with the vegetables, so he set his bowl aside. His family were strict Buddhists who did not eat the flesh of animals. But the bread was soft and warm, as though it had come straight from an oven, and the fruit was cool and luscious, as though it had been picked perfectly ripe. He had more than enough to satisfy his appetite.

Loki pushed his empty bowl aside. "Don't care for your stew?"

Yutang wondered how to explain, then settled for, "No."

Loki leaned forward to take Yutang's bowl. "Don't want our hosts to think we're not—" Loki slumped onto the table. Yutang's bowl fell on its side, spilling stew into the tight weaving of vines that made their table.

Yutang froze with fear. Was Loki dead? Then the Trickster snored loudly.

Yutang started to laugh in relief. Then he thought about being among strange people with strange powers. He said, "Loki?" and shook his arm. Loki continued to snore. Why would the Trickster fall asleep so quickly? Yutang came up with two answers: Either this was another of Loki's tricks or the elves had drugged the stew.

He glanced at the forest. He heard sounds like wind in the distance and a songbird's call. In the bright sunlight, the woods seemed safe. But this was a place where wolves ran free. And it was the home of creatures who could certainly turn themselves into wolves if they pleased.

He said, "Loki? If this is a trick to scare me, it has worked very well."

Loki rolled his head and stopped snoring. Yutang expected him to sit up. He began to drool onto the table. That was enough answer for Yutang. Loki was too vain to look so pathetic for a trick.

Yutang wanted to run into the woods and not stop running until he reached the open plains. But what was to say that he could make it through the forest, or that he would be any safer if he did? Could he carry Loki all that way? The Shapechanger may have been a small giant, but he made a large man. If only he had changed himself into something small before he had passed out!

The Pirate King would leave Loki and escape while he could, Yutang thought. Then he imagined returning to Asgard. "Where's Loki?" they would ask. He would say, "I left him." "Where's Thor's hammer?" they would ask next. He would say, "I do not know. I was afraid and ran away."

Yutang thought, *Running away will help no one. If I can find out why Brook and Birdsong tricked Loki, I might learn something that will help.* He sighed. *I am not the Pirate King. And that is best.* He let himself slump onto the table and began breathing slow, deep breaths.

The wicker surface of the table softened under his face. That seemed nice, until he felt something brush his ankles and wrists. He peeked between his eyelashes. The vines of the table and chair slowly grew over him and Loki like living ropes.

Yutang twisted, as if shifting in his sleep. The vines released him. But when he settled down, the vines began creeping over him again.

He made himself lie as still as Loki. How long would it take the vines to make him their prisoner? Before he could decide, two mountain lions padded into the glade. Though their hides were brown, their eyes were silver.

He wanted to scream and run. Ordinary mountain lions might be as wary of him as he was of them. But these two would probably enjoy chasing him. The mountain lions moved out of his sight. Their paws were too light on the grass for him to hear them. A breeze stirred the hair on the back of his neck. Was that a mountain lion's breath just before it bit?

Having something bad happen to you while you were pretending to be asleep would be as bad as having it happen while you *were* asleep. No, it would be worse. If you survived, you would feel like an idiot for lying there and letting yourself become a mountain lion's snack.

A cool hand touched his shoulder. He almost flinched, but somehow he didn't. Then he heard the soft voices of Birdsong and Brook.

"Loki had just escaped with Yggdrasill's acorn. Why did he return?"

"He's the Trickster. Who can know?"

"A tricked Trickster now."

"Perhaps he tries to trick us by pretending he's been tricked."

"Would you wake him and ask him?"

"And have him slip away as a fly or an ant? No. Let them both sleep here until Hel comes for them."

"Then we'll never learn where he put the acorn."

"The World Tree will drop another one in time. We're patient."

"Do you think the hammer is truly missing?"

"If that's not part of the Skytraveler's trick."

"Something should be done about Asgard, lest the wood be threatened again."

"The giants march. We might aid them."

"It is not our way to march to war."

"No, but we might turn our magic against Asgard. It has crops that could be made to die, trees that could be made to fall, water that could be turned bitter and foul. Their horses might attack their riders. Their dogs might attack their masters. Asgard was all forest once. It could be again."

The vines felt dangerously tight around Yutang's arms and legs. Afraid he had waited too long, he wrenched himself up. The vines scraped his skin, but they tore free. Yutang stood, shaking the vines away from him.

The elves stepped back from the table. No hint of amusement showed on their faces, only surprise and fear.

"Please!" Yutang said. "You—"

The elves disappeared. Yutang glanced around the glade. He and Loki were alone—unless the elves were still near, invisible or too small to see. "Loki has been with me since we left Asgard!" he said. "He could not have done what you think he did!"

No answer came. If the elves heard him, they had made up their minds. Perhaps they knew the answer to a thought that troubled him: Could Loki be in two places at once? That would be the greatest trick.

Yutang looked at Loki and then at the Sky-traveler's red boots. Would they fly for anyone else? Yutang stooped to pull off one of Loki's boots. The cloth felt soft and smooth and slightly warm. As he reached for the other boot, an idea struck him.

Leaving Loki with one boot, Yutang took off his own right boot, stuck it in his jacket pocket, and slipped on Loki's boot. Though the Trick-ster's feet were half again as large as Yutang's, the boot fit perfectly. Yutang nodded with satis-faction. Then he smiled, realizing that he had been in the lands of magic long enough that he would have been more surprised if a flying boot had *not* fit perfectly.

He stood and said, "Go, boot." Nothing hap-pened. "Up." Nothing. "Away." Nothing. "Gid-dyap." Nothing. He said the same things in Chi-nese. Still nothing. He hopped on one foot. The only result was the certainty that if the elves were spying on him, they would be sure he was an idiot.

Maybe he could only fly wearing both red boots. He started to reach for the other, then thought he heard something far off, like wind rustling leaves. The shadows under the trees seemed darker. Would the elves do something so he couldn't escape? He started to run toward the edge of the glade to see what he could and took one step in the red boot—

His foot slid ahead of him above the grass. He flailed his arms wildly to keep from falling backward. The boot scooted to the edge of the glade and stopped. Yutang flailed again to keep from falling forward. When he caught his balance, he looked into the woods.

Something moved in the distance. Something bulky and pale, followed by another, then a third, then four or five more. The nearest one crashed through a bush, and he saw it clearly. A pack of bears loped toward him. He could not tell how many there were in all. He could see their silver eyes, and that was all he needed to know.

He stepped toward Loki. The boot carried him back like a skate gliding over ice. He yanked the vines away from Loki, turned around, grabbed Loki's arms and pulled them up over his shoulders. With the Trickster leaning against his back, he looked at the top of a tree across the glade.

"Boots," he said aloud, because that helped him concentrate, "we're dragging Loki up there."

He stepped forward, trying to think only of the treetop where he wanted to go, trying to keep from wondering how near the bears were, trying to keep from remembering how heavy Loki was, trying to pull as hard as he could because there was no way to forget that the tall man must weigh two hundred pounds or more—

And Yutang and Loki slid through the air to the top of the tree. They tore through its highest branches, breaking twigs that scratched Yutang's face and hands and tore his clothes.

He looked back. The bears were turning into hawks.

Yutang leaned forward like a skier going downhill and thought that he was stepping to the horizon. He and Loki shot across the treetops.

The hawks pursued them. Yutang imagined what would happen if they caught up: beaks and talons tearing at his face, or a hawk landing on his shoulders to become something so heavy that the red boots would crash into the forest...

He glanced back. The hawks were falling behind.

From there, the flight across the forest was almost easy. He flew high to find the landmarks:

the plains, the river, the distant mountains. Once he decided where Asgard must be, he took a step toward it, and they flew.

As they traveled, he wondered about Loki and the elves. Even with one boot carrying half of the Trickster's weight, Loki was heavy and felt heavier with every minute. Yutang knew he would have to land several times on the way to rest. He didn't mind that. He only wished he had found Thor's hammer and hoped that Joshua or Toby had.

Flying past Vanaheim, he looked down at the city on the river. It would be beautiful when the Vanir finished rebuilding, but it would never be as beautiful as San Francisco, he thought. He wished he could see his home from the air.

He had decided to land and rest when he saw movement far ahead of him. The red boots carried him and Loki so fast that a single dark shape quickly became four, all headed straight toward him. Three raced along the ground, raising a dust cloud behind them. The fourth flew high above the others. Had the elves sent word for someone to catch them?

The four dark shapes came closer, close enough for Yutang to see them clearly. On the ground, a black-haired man rode an eight-legged gray stallion, a pale-haired man rode a glowing golden boar, and a pale-haired woman rode a giant black cat. Flying above and ahead of them, a white goat and a black one pulled a chariot that carried a red-bearded man, a gray dog, and two boys, one with light skin, one with dark.

"Yutang!" Joshua shouted.

"He's captured Loki!" Toby called.

"Where's my hammer?" demanded Thor.

Yutang called back, "The elves do not know!" He jerked his head downward. "I need to rest!"

He skidded to a stop on the grass in front of Tyr, Freyr, and Freyja, then lowered his burden to the ground. Freyr and Freyja gaped at the sleeping Trickster. Tyr laughed grimly and said, "We came to save you from him. It seems you saved us."

"From what?"

"A traitor took the hammer," Freyja said. "So Skrymir said, and there's no reason for him to lie about that."

Tyr said, "A thief who looked like me took the Dark Lady's necklace. One who looked like Thor took Skrymir's crown."

Yutang said, "The elves said Loki stole their acorn."

Thor leaped from his chariot as his goats landed near the other Aesir and Vanir. He glared at Loki. "Who else is so fond of making trouble?"

Toby, Joshua, and Lincoln jumped down after Thor. *We were glad to leave each other in Asgard,*

Yutang thought. *What can we say to each other now?* With the Norse gods talking of war, anything else would have to wait. Still, Yutang was glad when Lincoln trotted over to lick his hand.

"You did well," Freyja told Yutang.

"No," he answered, wishing he had. "The elves drugged Loki. All I did was escape."

"More than escape," said Thor. "You learned my hammer's not in Alfheim. And you brought Loki back."

Freyja knelt by the Trickster, touched her hand to his forehead, then stood. "It's elf magic. I can wake him. But it'll take a day or two."

"Which we don't have," said Freyr. "The giants will reach Asgard before sunset."

"And they'll regret that," Thor said with fury. "Even if I don't have my hammer."

Tyr shrugged. "They'll regret it. But not as much as we will."

Freyja said, "It seems the hammer's not in Jotunheim, Nidavellir, Svartalfheim, or Alfheim."

Joshua said, "Someone could be moving it to make it harder to find."

Thor raised his arm and shouted in a voice like thunder, "Mjollnir! To me!"

Yutang clapped his hands over his ears and saw the other boys do the same. When he uncovered his ears, he looked around, certain something must come of such a mighty yell.

Thor sighed. "No one moved it to Vanaheim or Asgard, or it would've come to me."

Toby asked, "Where's left to look, then?"

"Earth?" suggested Joshua.

Freyr answered, "Heimdall would've seen anyone who crossed the Bifrost Bridge. And Captain Malachi would know if anyone rode the *Basset*. There's no other way to Midgard."

"If there are nine worlds," Yutang said, "that leaves two."

Tyr nodded. "Niflheim and Muspellheim."

Freyja set her hand on the hilt of her sword. "The land of the dead and the land of the demons. Not much of a choice."

Thor said, "The demons lie beyond the land of the dead. Go to Hel first. If she doesn't have it, Surt must."

Tyr said, "If Surt has it, why hasn't he come?"

A deep horn sounded, at once far off and close, somehow sounding all around them.

"Heimdall calls," Freyja said. "We may be too late...."

The horn sounded again, a different note this time.

"Skrymir's army," Thor said. "No sign of Surt's demons."

"The elves want to help the giants," Yutang said.

Thor nodded grimly. "With such help, Skrymir may not need Surt."

Tyr said, "If Skrymir seems to be winning, Surt will come, no matter who has the hammer."

"We must return," Freyr said. "Asgard needs us."

"True words, Vanir," said Thor.

"No need for the boys to die with us," said Tyr. "Take them to the *Basset.*"

Freyja turned to them. "I'm sorry my prophecy brought you here—"

"I am not," Yutang said, surprising himself by speaking up as boldly as the Pirate King.

"Me, neither," agreed Toby.

"Maybe it's not too late," said Joshua. "We don't have to go yet—"

Heimdall's horn sounded again, three notes in a pattern that Yutang did not recognize.

"The Dark Lady's cavalry," Tyr said.

"There's no time to argue," Freyr told the boys. "You're not warriors!"

Knowing he could not quit now, Yutang looked at Freyja. "You said maybe we are here because warriors are not needed. I will keep looking."

"So'll I," said Joshua.

"Hey, you won't be rid of me so easily," said Toby.

Freyr said, "You can't go on without us."

"Of course they can," Thor said, turning to Joshua. "Take the chariot, lad. I'll fly back in Loki's boots." He stepped aside to stroke the goats between their horns and added, "Take good care of Tanngnost and Tanngrisni."

"I will," Joshua promised.

Tyr turned to Toby. "Tell the goats to take you to the *Basset,* and they will."

Toby shook his head. "One of us will find the hammer." He looked at Freyja. "Haven't your prophecies come true so far?"

She smiled sadly. "If Ragnarok is coming, you should be home, not here."

Toby opened his mouth to speak, then closed it and nodded. Joshua leaned down to stroke Lincoln's head. Yutang thought about his mother and father in Chinatown, and all the worlds ending. He knew then that he could not go home until the hammer was found or Asgard fell.

Tyr jumped down from the saddle, then threw Loki over Sleipnir's back. "A shame he won't be awake to see what he's done."

"True." Thor began pulling off his boots. As Yutang moved upwind of the smell of the thunder god's feet, Thor added, "Maybe you can wake him before it ends. I want to see his face when he learns that he hasn't escaped the final battle."

14
THE HAMMER

Joshua jumped up into Thor's chariot. Toby and
Yutang scrambled after him. Last came Lincoln,
who stood with his paws up on the side of the
chariot and barked once at Freyja's giant cat.

Joshua took a deep breath, then picked up
the reins. It was one thing to ride in the thunder
god's chariot, but to drive it? Everyone—the two
Aesir, the two Vanir, the two boys, even the eight-
legged horse and the golden boar—was watching him. Well, he'd driven cart horses and oxen
and mules, and Thor's goats were smarter than
any of those. Joshua shook the chariot's reins
and shouted, "Ho, Tanngnost! Ho, Tanngrisni! To
Niflheim!"

The goats leaped forward in their harness.
Wooden wheels bounced across the plain, jarring
the riders and shaking the chariot. Toby and

Yutang both grabbed Lincoln to keep the dog from skidding off.

Then the ride became perfectly smooth. The sky wrapped itself around them. The ground dropped farther and farther below. Joshua glanced down. Thor, Tyr, Freyja, and Freyr were already racing back toward the mountains and Asgard. He looked up. The sun was still high overhead. How much time had passed since leaving the *Basset*? Maybe the winter sun set later in the lands of Norse myth. He wasn't even sure it *was* winter here.

Toby cleared his throat and said, "I was thinking—"

Joshua said, "*Mighty* surprising things happen here."

Toby glanced at him, and Joshua realized that Toby might not know that his words were meant as a friendly joke. But before Joshua could say anything more, Toby laughed. "Fair enough. And what surprising things happened to you since you left us?"

Yutang nodded and said, "I, too, would like to know."

So Joshua told about Jotunheim and Skrymir's fury over his crown. Then Toby told about Svartalfheim and the Dark Lady's anger over her necklace. Both boys told about going back to find Asgard bustling with preparations for war. Thor and Joshua had wanted to find Loki before he could harm Yutang, and so they had set out with Tyr, Freyr, and Freyja.

Joshua looked at Yutang. "You were lucky."

"Perhaps," Yutang agreed. "But Loki had chances to hurt me, and did not." He told about Alfheim and the forest elves' displeasure over their acorn.

When Yutang finished, Joshua said, "It doesn't add up."

"No," Yutang agreed. "Loki likes some mean tricks. But I do not think he would hurt his family."

Toby stared at him. "To be sure, he's so fond of his giant wife and three monster children that he lives far from them in Asgard."

Yutang shook his head. "He has another wife now, and two boys. He told me. They live in Asgard."

Joshua cut in. "What I can't figure is why the hammer would be with Hel or Surt."

Toby said, "Because it's nowhere else. That's what they all decided."

Joshua shook his head. "But if Surt had it, he'd be attacking Asgard already, right? And if Hel had it, she'd just give it to Surt, right? It's got to be somewhere else."

Toby asked, "And where wouldn't they think to look?"

Yutang frowned. "A place so frightening that they would not imagine anyone would go into it?"

Toby stared at Joshua. "Loki's children. The serpent's in the sea around Midgard. Heimdall would've seen anyone go there. But the wolf, Fenrir, that bit off Tyr's hand—" Toby swallowed. "He's under an island named Lyngvi. Any idea where that is?"

Joshua looked at the others. "No, but we can get there. If that's what we want." Yutang nodded. Toby looked down at his maimed hand, then nodded, too. Joshua called, "Tanngnost! Tanngrisni! To Lyngvi!"

The goats veered, whipping the chariot around, then raced on. Ahead, between the green of the plains and the blue of the sky, lay the dark strip of the sea.

As they flew over the water, a mist grew thickly around them. No one talked. Joshua hoped they'd made the right decision. Even if they had, would they be too late? What would Fenrir be like, if he frightened the Aesir? Joshua patted Lincoln's head for comfort, then looked at Toby and Yutang. They stared out into the gray clouds surrounding them. *At least*, he thought, *I'm not going alone*.

Black rocks suddenly rose out of the mist before them. Joshua shouted, "Hang on!" The wheels bounced, the boys rocked, and then the goats stood still and looked back at them with an impatient expression.

"Lava," Yutang said, looking at the dark stone surface beneath them. "I think."

Nothing grew there. The only sounds were the cold wind and large waves beating against rocks. Lincoln pressed against Joshua's legs and made a whimper of concern, as if he thought they should be anywhere but Lyngvi.

Toby grinned nervously and said, "Sure, I'd overlook this place myself, if I could."

"Me too," Joshua agreed, forcing a smile. He stroked Lincoln's back and wondered if he did that for the dog's sake or his own.

Yutang stepped down. The black rocks crunched beneath his boots. He pointed at a darker shape within a dark cliff that rose nearby. "A cave."

"All right," said Toby, jumping down after him.

Joshua told Lincoln, "We'll be back," and followed the others. "We should've brought torches."

Yutang peered into the mouth of the cave. "We may not need them."

Joshua caught up. Deep in the darkness, he could see a red glow. Warm air blew steadily from the cave.

Toby said, "I wondered if this was the land of

the dead. Now I'm thinking it's the land of the demons."

Joshua glanced around. "Whatever it is, we're alone."

"Listen," said Yutang.

From within the cave came a long, angry howl.

"Fenrir," said Toby.

Joshua saw both boys looking at him. "Then we're where we want to be," he said, and headed toward the dim red glow.

They stumbled into the dark cave. Joshua took each step expecting something terrible to be there. He held his hands in front of his face to keep from bumping into anything. He thought of what his fingers might touch—skeletons, monsters, soft decaying muck that would cling to his skin, hard jagged things that would slice him. All he felt was warm, rough stone. There were no spiderwebs, no sleeping bats. Nothing that lived was in this place, except the wolf that howled far below.

The cave forked. Two tunnels led down, each proceeding toward the warm red glow. Joshua stopped. Toby and Yutang both bumped into him. "What is it?" Toby whispered.

Before Joshua could answer, he heard something behind them. Claws clicked lightly on stone. He had barely enough time to think they were trapped. Then he recognized the new-comer's breathing and called, "Lincoln!" The old dog jumped up to lick his face. Joshua grinned in the darkness. "I thought you were going to stay behind."

Yutang said, "Which way do we go?"

Joshua listened. The wolf roared again. The sound echoed all around them. It could have come from either tunnel.

Lincoln growled at the right-hand path. The roar came again, louder. With a sinking feeling, Joshua realized that Fenrir knew they were coming.

"This way," Joshua said, heading toward the right. Lincoln barked at him. Joshua said, "I know we shouldn't go this way. That's why we have to."

After several steps, Lincoln quit warning him and trotted on. When they came to the next fork, Lincoln growled at the path leading straight ahead, and they headed down it.

The red glow grew brighter as the air grew warmer. Joshua opened his jacket and undid the top buttons of his shirt. The roaring became so loud that it hurt his ears.

The glow came from lava flowing out of the side of a cavern and falling into a crevasse so deep that he could not see its bottom. Near the edge of the cavern lay a dark gray mound—or so

Joshua thought until it roared and lunged for him. He saw red eyes as big as a Viking's shield, teeth as big as Thor's forearm, a throat large enough to swallow him in a gulp—

Toby and Yutang yanked him back. Toby pointed past the enormous wolf. A slender chain fastened it to a huge boulder. Beside the boulder, where someone with sufficient strength could have thrown it, lay a hammer with a carved golden head and a short wooden handle. The hammer shone with a flickering blue-white light, as if it had lightning inside it trying to get out.

"Maybe we don't have to get it ourselves," said Toby. "All we're supposed to do is find it."

Yutang said, "If we go back without it, the war may begin."

"May've begun anyway," said Joshua. A lean gray shape darted past him, heading for Fenrir. "No, Lincoln!" he shouted. "Come back!"

Fenrir's huge head turned toward Lincoln, then the wolf charged the dog. Lincoln veered to follow the cavern wall without slowing. Joshua chased him, calling, "Lincoln! Stop!" His only thought was that the gray dog was too old and too slow to dodge Fenrir's flashing teeth.

Lincoln sprang sideways as Fenrir's jaws snapped. Joshua's heart fell with the certainty that bravery could not make up for speed or strength. Then Fenrir's golden chain pulled tight, jerking the wolf back. For an instant, Joshua's heart soared—cleverness could make up for speed and strength. Then he heard Lincoln yip in pain and saw the dog's tail in Fenrir's mouth. Cleverness was not always enough. Fenrir turned his head, dragging Lincoln back to him.

Joshua leaped forward, grabbed Lincoln by both front legs, and yanked with all his strength. Lincoln yelped again, then scrambled away from Fenrir. Joshua pulled the dog into his arms and ran several steps back, expecting the wolf to lunge for them.

But the wolf had wheeled around. It loped back toward the boulder where its chain was fastened. Toby was there, picking up the hammer and a sack that lay beside it.

"Run!" Joshua shouted. "It's coming!"

Toby glanced up. His face looked paler than ever as he began to run back with his heavy load. But Fenrir ran faster.

"Here!" Yutang shouted as he raced straight at the wolf. "Here, stupid monster! Chinese food tastes best!"

Fenrir looked from Toby to Yutang, who was closer, then turned. Yutang spun around, but his boot slipped on the rock. Then he caught himself and began running back, with Fenrir close behind. Too close, Joshua thought, as the wolf snapped at Yutang's queue, nearly catching it.

Joshua snatched up a rock, ran forward, and threw it, hitting Fenrir hard in the ribs. "Good Southern vittles!" he shouted, jumping up and down. "Nothing goes down better!"

The wolf turned again and lunged. Joshua leaped away, fell, and rolled across the rocks, not daring to take time to stand. He heard the wolf's claws clatter across the stone, coming closer and closer, then heard "Fenrir, you great fool, it's a fine Irish feast just waiting for you!"

The claws slowed for a moment. Joshua didn't, and then he was against the side of the cavern, safely out of Fenrir's range, with Lincoln licking his face.

The boys and the dog ran from the cave, with Fenrir roaring his frustration. In the chariot, Toby dropped the golden hammer and the sack, then said, "Lincoln's bleeding. An awful lot."

"Fenrir bit off his tail." Joshua tossed the reins to Yutang. "You got this flying thing down pretty good."

Yutang nodded, shook the reins, and shouted, "Ho, Tanngnost! Ho, Tanngrisni! To Odin's hall in Asgard!"

The goats jerked the chariot away from the island of Lyngvi as Joshua stroked Lincoln's side and said, "Lie calm. You'll be fine. I never had a tail, and it hasn't hurt me a bit."

"Here," Toby said.

Joshua looked up. The Irish boy shivered, bare-chested in the wind, holding out his shirt. Joshua took it, tore it into strips, and began bandaging his dog.

Yutang said, "Will he be all right?"

"He's old," Joshua said, trying to sound as though he weren't worried so Lincoln wouldn't be upset. The dog kept trying to sit up. Joshua kept pushing him down, saying, "Lie still. Don't want to get blood all over Mr. Thor's chariot."

He knotted the bandages around the stump of Lincoln's tail. Lincoln immediately began to push feebly at the bandages with his nose, so Joshua sat and wrapped his arms around him. Lincoln lifted his head as if that was a very hard thing to do and licked Joshua's face. Joshua began to cry then.

Lincoln rested his head in Joshua's lap. Joshua watched the dog's ribs rise and fall. His breathing slowed, and then it seemed to settle as he slept. Joshua wiped his tears on his sleeve and looked up.

At the reins, Yutang glanced down and said, "That is a good dog. He could guard the emperor in the Forbidden City."

Joshua nodded.

Toby had put his jacket back on. He said, "I've been thinking some more. I want you both to know that I'd be sorry for flinging stones and fighting with you on the wharf if it weren't for two things."

"What's that?" asked Joshua, wishing for a second that they had left Toby on Lyngvi.

"I wouldn't be here, and I wouldn't have met you. You're fine, brave lads, the pair of you, as good as any boy I know and maybe better." He knelt and scratched behind Lincoln's ear. "And Yutang's right. Lincoln's a great dog. Great as the Irish heroes' dogs."

Joshua nodded.

Yutang said, "I, too, am grateful for knowing both of you. It could be a fine thing to be a barbarian."

Joshua looked at the boys. They wanted him to say something, he knew, something that would mean he didn't hold a grudge against them. He liked them both. But he blamed them, too, for pulling him into this and getting Lincoln hurt—

Lincoln had opened his eyes and was licking Toby's hand. "Shoot," Joshua said. "For a pair of fools, you're not so bad."

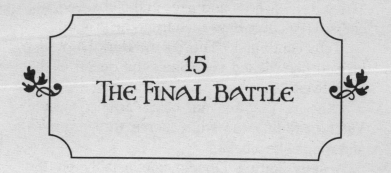

15
THE FINAL BATTLE

Riding the chariot toward Asgard, Toby worried about Lincoln, even though Joshua's dog seemed to be feeling better, and about the prophecy, even though they had the hammer. When he looked over the side of the chariot, he saw his second fear coming true. "Ah, no! We're too late!"

"What is it?" Joshua asked from the deck of the chariot, where he sat with Lincoln.

"The fight's all but started. The armies are moving. There's a great ugly fellow the size of a mountain out front of one, all in silver armor."

"That's Skrymir," said Joshua, "the king of the giants."

"Then those would be his subjects, the great ugly louts behind him. There are an awful lot of them," Toby added, wishing he could sound more hopeful.

Yutang spoke up, not sounding hopeful at all. "They have swords and axes and clubs—no, not clubs. Trees they have torn from the ground."

Toby continued, "There's the Dark Lady, bad luck to her wicked self. She's the queen of the dark elves."

"She is the one in black armor?" asked Yutang. "Riding the white horse with red eyes and wings like a bat's?"

Joshua settled Lincoln comfortably on the chariot floor and stood up beside the other boys.

Toby saw from Joshua's face that it was worse than he had imagined. The giants were too big and too numerous for anyone to hope to stop. And the Dark Lady was awful, like seeing Death riding toward you. Following her were a cavalry of pale men and women, some with lances, some holding bows and arrows.

"Who are those folks on foot beside the Dark Lady?" Joshua asked, pointing.

Yutang made a noise that was almost a growl. "Birdsong and Brook and more light elves. The ones who tried to capture Loki and me." There were a hundred or more of them, dressed entirely in dull white, the color of bones and dead wood. Where they passed, the green grass of the plain was withering and turning brown.

Across the field from them, the Aesir and their Vanir allies came, armed and ready. Odin rode Sleipnir and carried a long spear with a golden head. Freyja stood in a chariot drawn by four large black cats. Freyr, on golden Gullinbursti, held a flashing sword. Tyr and Heimdall rode with them. So did others that Toby remembered from Odin's hall when the boys had first come to Asgard.

The Aesir and Vanir were clearly outnumbered, but they moved forward as bravely as the giants and elves that opposed them. If Toby only looked at the gods, he could be optimistic: They were so marvelous, so full of magic, that surely they could defeat anything. But when he compared them, so small and so few, to their enemies, he knew this must be Ragnarok, whether Surt came or not.

Thor walked beside Odin. He carried a thick bundle of spears over one shoulder and wore a heavy sword on each hip. He must have seen Heimdall look upward, because he was the first to call up to them. "It's too late, lads! Go home while you can!"

Joshua shouted, "No, it's not!"

Toby hoped Joshua was right. He lifted the heavy golden hammer in both hands and dropped it over the side of the chariot.

Thor stared, then laughed, dropped his spears, ripped off his sword belt, and leaped thirty feet into the air to catch the hammer as it fell. When he landed, he brought the hammer down on the ground with both hands.

The field buckled and rolled as if an earth-quake had struck. A cry of despair came from the invading army. Joshua looked to see if they would run away. Instead, they ran faster toward Asgard's defenders.

"Thor's hammer isn't enough!" Yutang shouted.

That couldn't be. They couldn't have faced Fenrir and still not have stopped the end of the world. Toby looked away from the battlefield—and saw the sack he'd grabbed in Fenrir's cave.

He tugged it open. In the bottom lay a bright circle of gold, a cold-looking silver chain with a dark stone hanging from it, and a little brown acorn.

Joshua looked over Toby's shoulder. "Well, I'll be," he breathed.

"Get us to the giants! Hurry!" Toby called to Yutang.

Yutang shouted, "Tanngnost! Tanngrisni!" He turned the goats toward the giants, and the char-iot raced their way.

Skrymir scowled at them, lifted his sword in both hands, and shouted, "Do you think we're cowards to flee before the hammer! We'll fight!"

"Why?" Joshua shouted. "Here's your crown!"

Toby reached into the sack and drew out the

golden ring. It was too small to be the crown, but it couldn't be anything else. He had to pray they had guessed right. He threw it over the side toward Skrymir. The ring expanded as it fell, growing large enough to fence in ten cows, and landed on Skrymir's head.

"And your necklace!" Joshua shouted as Yutang turned the goats toward the Dark Lady. Toby threw the silver chain toward her. She caught it in her hand, then raised one pale eyebrow.

"And your acorn!" Joshua shouted as Yutang turned the goats again. Toby threw the acorn to Birdsong and Brook. The male elf caught it. Toby saw nothing special about it, but all the light elves smiled as if a child had been returned to them.

Yutang brought the chariot down between the armies. Thor ran up and stroked the goats' muzzles, then told the boys, "You did well. Who gets our thanks?"

"It's too soon to thank anyone," boomed Skrymir. "You say Asgard is not to blame. But those are only words."

Toby looked around. The chariot was surrounded by Aesir and Vanir on one side, giants and elves and dark elves on the other.

"This is Loki's fault," said Thor, scowling.

"You think he wouldn't brag of that to his

father if it was true?" Skrymir asked.

Thor stared at him. "You claimed there was a traitor."

Skrymir nodded. "Who told me the hammer was gone. Not who took it."

"Name the traitor!" Thor demanded as lightning flashed across the skies.

"Why should I?" Skrymir asked. "He may be of use to me again."

"You don't have to name him," Joshua said, and everyone stared as he bent down to stroke Lincoln. The old dog rose unsteadily, but he stood. Joshua held out the sack that had contained the crown, the necklace, and the acorn. Lincoln sniffed it.

"Whose is it, boy? Find him!"

Lincoln stepped away from the chariot. He sniffed the air, looked at Skrymir, then the Dark Lady, then Birdsong and Brook.

Then he turned and walked toward Odin. Freyja gasped, and Thor said, "What's this?"

"Trust him," Odin said, drawing the reins to move Sleipnir aside. And Lincoln passed Odin to stop in front of Freyr on his golden boar.

"Brother?" Freyja said as though she could not believe it.

Freyr stared at them all. He opened his mouth to speak but, looking at Freyja, he closed his mouth and looked down at his hands.

"How could you?" Freyja asked. "We made peace—"

"Because we had no choice!" Freyr shouted. "The Aesir should suffer! Like we Vanir suffered at their hands!"

"We all suffered," Freyja said.

Thor said, "You would have brought Ragnarok?"

Freyr shook his head. "Surt would never have found the hammer. I hid it where no one would have." He looked at the boys. "If not for them."

Tyr said, "You expect us to be grateful that you wished to destroy only Asgard and not the other worlds?"

Freyr glanced at the war god, then drew on Gullinbursti's reins. The boar wheeled and charged away so quickly that mount and rider became a blur streaking across the field.

Odin and Sleipnir lunged after them. Now they would learn which was faster, Toby thought, Freyr's boar or Odin's horse.

Thor threw his hammer. It struck the earth in front of Gullinbursti's hooves in a crack of lightning and thunder, opening a chasm forty feet wide. Freyr turned back, trapped, as the hammer returned to Thor's hand.

Odin raised his golden spear and drew it back, ready to throw.

Joshua shouted, "No!"

Odin's gray eye flicked to Joshua. Then Odin nodded and lowered the spear. "There has been no killing this day. But what should we do with him?"

Joshua turned to Toby and Yutang. Yutang shook his head. Toby looked at the others around him. When he studied Freyja's face, Toby knew what he would want, in her place. And he said, "Send him home."

"Is that punishment?" said Skrymir.

"He'll be ashamed of his deeds," said Birdsong and Brook.

"That is cold punishment," said the Dark Lady.

Odin nodded and looked at Freyr. "Go."

Freyr sat still, his eyes locked with Freyja's. She shook her head and said, "They're only our enemies as long as we hate them."

The armies of the Aesir, the Vanir giants, light elves, and dark elves parted. Freyr turned Gullinbursti and rode slowly away.

"A sad time," said Odin. "But it could have been much sadder. To whom do we owe our thanks?"

Toby glanced at Joshua and Yutang. To his surprise, neither of them spoke up. After a moment of thought, he stepped forward.

"Ah." Tyr nodded. "Bravely done, Toby of

Midgard."

"No," Toby said. "All I did was grab the hammer. Fenrir would've gotten me if Yutang hadn't distracted him."

Freyja smiled at Yutang. "I congratulate you."

Yutang shook his head. "But Fenrir would have gotten *me* if Joshua had not distracted him."

Thor grinned at Joshua. "I thought it'd be you."

As everyone stared at Joshua, he said, "Fenrir would've gotten *me* if Toby hadn't distracted him. So we're back to Toby."

"We're not," Toby insisted. "I would've gone to see Hel and Surt if Joshua hadn't figured out that the hammer was elsewhere."

"But I wouldn't have known where if you hadn't thought of Fenrir," Joshua answered.

Toby said, "But I wouldn't have thought of that if Yutang hadn't realized it must be someplace frightful."

Yutang shrugged. "Anyone could think of that."

"But you did," Toby said, pleased at finding the solution. "So Yutang must be the one."

Yutang shook his head. "It makes as much sense to think it is me as to think it is..." Yutang looked at the gray dog who had come with them from San Francisco.

Toby saw it all clearly then. "Lincoln discovered the traitor!"

"And showed us the way to Fenrir!" Yutang added.

"And distracted him in the first place!" Joshua noted. "And when I saw Yutang in San Francisco for the first time, it was because Lincoln wandered toward him."

"Huh," said Toby. "The first time I saw Yutang, it was because I heard a dog bark in his direction."

Freyja smiled at them. "If none of you will accept our thanks, we will certainly give it to Lincoln."

"All we may give are words," said Odin. "Nothing you can take back to your world."

"Words, and a bit more." Thor stooped, scratched behind both of Lincoln's ears, and laughed as Lincoln licked his face.

"Perhaps more even than that." Freyja put her hand on Lincoln's head. Her face became somber, and when she spoke, her voice seemed deeper than before. "There shall be many years of happy life for the one who saved the Aesir, for three good friends shall care for him. One shall be honored as a teacher, one as a leader, and one for a simple life that will cause all who know him to love him."

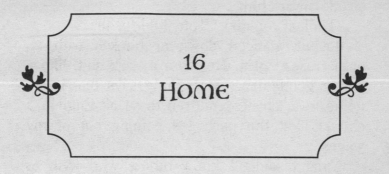

16
Home

Yutang stood on the wharf and watched the sun set into the sea. The Pirate King would want to be sailing into that sunset, but Yutang was pleased to stay behind in San Francisco. The *Basset* had brought them back to the wharf shortly after they had left, just as Captain Malachi had promised. The boys had separated soon after that to go back to their daily lives. Now Yutang wondered, *Will Toby and Joshua be able to meet me?*

He didn't wonder long. He heard his name called far behind him. "Yutang!"

He turned to see Toby wave as he walked toward him. Yutang waved back, then heard a bark and turned the other way. Lincoln ran up to him and jumped up to rest his paws on his chest. Yutang laughed and scratched the gray dog behind the ears. Then he smiled as Joshua strode toward him.

"Look at you now," Toby told Joshua.

Joshua glanced down at himself with an embarrassed grin. He wore a dark suit, like a young gentleman. "Mrs. Fung says that if I'm going to teach her children to speak English, I should look the part. It's coming out of my wages."

Yutang said, "I know others who wish to speak like Americans."

Joshua nodded. "Mrs. Fung says she'll recommend me to all her friends. If you hadn't introduced us—"

Yutang shrugged. "If you hadn't been able to help her, my introduction would not have mattered."

Joshua turned to Toby. "So. Did you walk out of work?"

Toby laughed. "Ah, you should've seen it. I thought it'd be me and O'Hara alone on the sidewalk, but the whole factory followed me! Elizabeth O'Leary said it was the bravest thing she'd ever seen. Littleton cursed and swore. It'll make no difference. Everyone's standing fast. If he wants to keep his business going, he'll be paying us two dollars more a week, and letting us quit at five o'clock besides." Toby shook his head, then grinned at Yutang. "And how did it go for you?"

"I told my parents that San Francisco is my home," Yutang said. "I said they could save their money if they wanted, but for them. Because if I ever go to China, it will be to visit, not to stay. My mother cried, and my father would not talk to me for two hours. But when I left, she whispered to me that this is her home, too. And my father said that boys may not know what they want, but men do."

Toby and Joshua nodded and smiled. But before they could say anything more, Lincoln barked.

Yutang glanced down. Maybe it was his imagination. Yet if anyone asked him, he would swear that since they returned from Asgard, Lincoln's coat had become several shades darker, and he moved as easily as a young hound.

Yutang looked where Lincoln faced, out toward the sea. Far in the distance, a small ship with three masts sailed away from San Francisco. And maybe it wasn't the *Basset,* but all three boys waved just the same.

A NOTE
FROM THE AUTHOR

I can't remember when I first read about the Norse myths. I know that I always loved them. I read everything in the mythology section of the school library, followed the adventures of Thor in his comic book, and saw every Viking movie I could.

When I decided to write this story, I read a few more books to refresh my memory. My favorite reference was Kevin Crossley-Holland's *The Norse Myths.* But he should not be blamed for anything I did once the research was over and the writing began.

Bon voyage!

Will Shetterly

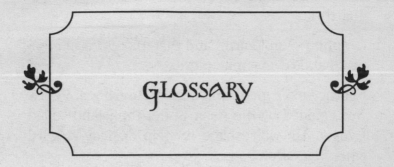

GLOSSARY

Author's note: All of these names are translated from Old Norse. That means that unless you're speaking Old Norse, you're free to pronounce them any way you like. For some of the trickier names, I've made suggestions. But if you come up with something you like better, that's fine. Perhaps the only important thing to remember is that *j* can be pronounced as a *y*.

Aesir *(ay-zeer)*: The gods of Asgard. Odin is their leader.

Alfheim *(alf-hime)*: The home of the light elves.

Angrboda *(an-gur-bo-duh)*: Loki's giant wife, who gave birth to Fenrir, Jormungand, and Hel.

Asgard: The home of the Aesir.

Bifrost: The rainbow bridge connecting Asgard and the Earth (and other worlds, too). Heimdall guards it.

Draupnir: A gold armband that makes eight identical bands every nine nights.

Fenrir: Loki's giant wolf son by Angrboda. Fenrir was chained by the Aesir under the island called Lyngvi. He will escape to help destroy Asgard when Ragnarok comes.

Fimbulvetr *(fim-bul-vet-ur)*: A terrible three-year-long winter that will come just before Ragnarok.

Fjorgyn *(fyor-gin)*: An earth-goddess, also known as Jord and Earth. Mother of Thor.

Freki: One of Odin's two wolves. The other is Geri.

Freyja *(frey-juh* or *frey-uh)*: Female Vanir goddess of fertility. Sister of Freyr and daughter of Njord. She rides to battle in a chariot pulled by cats.

Freyr *(frair* or *frey-ur)*: Male Vanir god of fertility. Brother of Freyja and son of Njord. He has a magic ship called *Skidbladnir* and a magic golden boar named Gullinbursti.

Frigg: Odin's Aesir wife.

Geri: One of Odin's two wolves. The other is Freki.

Gjall (*gyall* or *gjall*): Heimdall's horn. When blown, it can be heard in all nine worlds.

Gullinbursti: A golden boar made by dwarves. Loki gave it to Freyr as a present.

Gungnir: A spear that never misses. Loki got it from the dwarves and gave it to Odin.

Heimdall (*hime-doll*): Guardian of Bifrost and owner of the horn, Gjall.

Hel: Loki's daughter who rules Niflheim, the land of the dead. Half of her body is dead.

Huginn: A raven whose name means *thought*. Stays near Odin with another raven named Muninn.

Jarnsaxa: Thor's giant wife, mother of two of his sons, Modi and Magni.

Jormungand: Also known as the Midgard Serpent. Loki and Angrboda's serpent son who encircles the Earth and bites his tail.

Jotunheim (*jot-un-hime*): Home of the giants.

Kvasir (*kuh-va-zeer*): Vanir god of wisdom and poetry.

Loki: Odin's foster brother and Skrymir's son. Also known as the Trickster, the Skytraveler, and the Shape-changer. A giant who lives in

Asgard with the Aesir.

Lyngvi *(ling-vee)*: The island beneath which Fenrir is chained.

Magni: A son of Thor and Jarnsaxa, brother of Modi.

Midgard: Earth. Also known as "the middle world."

Mjollnir *(myoll-nur)*: A magic hammer that was made by dwarves. Loki gave it to Thor.

Modi: A son of Thor and Jarnsaxa, brother of Magni.

Muninn: A raven whose name means *memory.* Stays near Odin with another raven named Huginn.

Muspellheim: Home of fire demons, ruled by the giant demon Surt.

Narvi: Loki and Sigyn's son. His brother is Vali.

Nidavellir: Land of dwarves.

Niflheim: Home of the dead.

Njord *(nyord)*: Vanir god of wind and sea. Father of Freyr and Freyja.

Norns: Three sisters—Urd, Skuld, and Verdandi—who see the future.

Odin: The one-eyed ruler of the Aesir, father of Thor. Also known as the Allfather.

Ragnarok: The final battle between the gods and the giants, when all the worlds are destroyed.

Sif: Thor's Aesir wife. Her hair is made of gold.

Sigyn *(sig-inn)*: Loki's Aesir wife.

Skidbladnir: Freyr's ship that can be folded up and put into a pocket.

Skrymir: The enormous king of the giants of Jotunheim. Also known as Utgard-Loki.

Sleipnir *(sleep-nur)*: Odin's eight-legged horse.

Surt: Giant demon who rules Muspellheim.

Svartalfheim *(svart-alf-hime)*: Land of the dark elves.

Tanngnost: One of two goats that pull Thor's chariot.

Tanngrisni: One of two goats that pull Thor's chariot.

Thor: God of thunder and the sky. Son of Odin and Fjorgyn. Master of the hammer Mjollnir.

Thrud: Daughter of Thor and Sif.

Tyr: God of war. Son of Odin.

Utgard: City of the giants.

Valaskjalf *(vuh-lask-yalf* or *vuh-lask-jalf)*: Odin's hall.

Vali: Loki and Sigyn's son. His brother is Narvi.

Vanaheim: Home of the Vanir.

Vanir *(vuh-neer)*: The gods of Vanaheim. Once enemies of Asgard, they are now the Aesir's closest allies.

Yggdrasill *(igg-druh-sill)*: The World Tree that grows into all the nine worlds.

ABOUT THE AUTHOR

WILL SHETTERLY is a writer who enjoys exploring the shadowy boundary between our world and the next. Among his many works are two novels for the Borderlands series, *Elsewhere* and *Nevernever.*

For more information,
visit Will Shetterly's Web site:

www.player.org/pub/flash/people/will.html

Books by Tamora Pierce

THE SONG OF THE LIONESS QUARTET
Alanna: The First Adventure
In the Hand of the Goddess
The Woman Who Rides Like a Man
Lioness Rampant

THE IMMORTALS QUARTET
Wild Magic
Wolf-Speaker
Emperor Mage
The Realms of the Gods

PROTECTOR OF THE SMALL
First Test
Page

Books by Carol Hughes
Toots and the Upside-Down House
Jack Black and the Ship of Thieves